Here she was—neat, precise, always in control Nina Grant—pulling up to the gates of a compound with a man packing some sort of lethal weapon that couldn't be discovered by a pat-down.

Never, ever, in her wildest imagination would she have pictured herself in this situation.

Twisting in her seat, she skimmed a nervous glance over his knit shirt and pleated slacks. She couldn't spot any bulges. Except one, and that was right where it should be. Hastily, she raised her eyes.

"Are you sure they won't find anything?"

"Relax, Nina. We're being watched, remember?"

"Like I could forget?"

He shifted and stretched an arm along the back of her seat. Those blue eyes lanced into her. "You're wound tight, aren't you? You need a distraction."

She could have pulled back. His hold was loose enough, his intention clear. Sheer surprise held her still…coupled with an overwhelming and completely irrational hunger to feel his mouth on hers.

Dear Reader,

Have you ever planned the perfect vacation, only to
have one disaster after another occur? That's what
happened when we jaunted down to Cabo San Lucas
with our best pals, Neta and Dave. But even disasters
can turn into fun with the right attitude—and they
make terrific fodder for books!

I hope you enjoy this, the latest in my *Code Name:
Danger* series. And be sure to check my Web site at
www.merlinelovelace.com for news, information,
contests and releases yet to come.

Merline Lovelace

Merline Lovelace

Risky Engagement

ROMANTIC
SUSPENSE

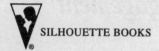

SILHOUETTE BOOKS

ISBN-13: 978-0-373-27683-7

RISKY ENGAGEMENT

Recycling programs for this product may not exist in your area.

Recent Books by Merline Lovelace

Silhouette Romantic Suspense

*Diamonds Can
   Be Deadly* #1411
Closer Encounters #1439
Stranded with a Spy #1483
Match Play #1500
Undercover Wife #1531
*Seduced by
   the Operative* #1589
Risky Engagement #1613

*Code Name: Danger
**Holidays Abroad
†Time Raiders

Silhouette Desire

*Devlin and the Deep
   Blue Sea* #1726
**The CEO's Christmas
   Proposition* #1905
**The Duke's New Year's
   Resolution* #1913
**The Executive's
   Valentine Seduction* #1917

Silhouette Nocturne

Mind Games #37
†*Time Raiders:
   The Protector* #75

MERLINE LOVELACE

A retired Air Force officer, Merline Lovelace served at bases all over the world, including tours in Taiwan, Vietnam and at the Pentagon. When she hung up her uniform for the last time, she decided to combine her love of adventure with a flair for storytelling, basing many of her tales on her experiences in the service.

Since then, she's produced more than eighty action-packed novels, many of which have made *USA TODAY* and Waldenbooks bestseller lists. More than ten million copies of her works are in print in thirty countries. Named Oklahoma's Writer of the Year and the Oklahoma Female Veteran of the Year, Merline is also a recipient of Romance Writers of America's prestigious RITA® Award.

To our great friends and traveling buds,
Neta and Dave. Didn't I warn you when we were on
our fourth rental car in as many days down in Cabo
that it would all end up in a book? Here's to many
more such grand misadventures!

Prologue

Sweat trickled down his temple, into his eye. Impatiently, Wolf blinked it away. He and his team had kept the hacienda perched atop a sun-baked cliff under surveillance for two days and two long nights now. From all indications, the bastard who owned it would make his move soon. And when he did, Wolf would take him down.

In the meantime, he was close to broiling under the afternoon sun. Summers in this corner of Mexico's Los Cabos Peninsula could be brutal. October wasn't much better. It didn't help that the azure sea shimmered in the distance, making a mockery of the sweat plastering his camouflage shirt to his back and—

"El Lobo!"

The low exclamation brought his gaze whipping to the man stretched out a few feet away on the dry, baked earth. He was one of Mexico's elite, handpicked by Wolf's counterpart for this op. Like Wolf, he was covered from head to toe in desert fatigues and dripping in sweat.

"Someone comes," he whispered urgently. "A woman. Not from here, I think."

He edged to one side so Wolf could take his place at the high-powered scope. Tripod mounted and over a foot long when fully extended, the scope packed almost enough power to pick out Neil Armstrong's footprints on the moon. More than enough to display in startlingly precise detail, the female trudging along the unpaved road leading to the hacienda they were keeping under surveillance.

His jaw locked, Wolf catalogued sweat-streaked, honey-brown hair showing beneath a wide-brimmed straw hat. Oversize designer sunglasses hid the upper half her face, but the lower half showed a mouth set in tight lines. A rumpled linen sundress in a pale green color, bared shoulders showing the first flush of sunburn.

"That's it," Wolf growled, when she paused at the gate cut into the high walls surrounding the hacienda's vast acreage and tipped her sun glasses to peer at the phone box beside the gate. "Com'on, *chica*. Take 'em off and give me a good target."

He centered the crosshairs on her face. Slowly, so slowly, she slid the glasses down an inch. Two. With a grunt of satisfaction, Wolf nailed her.

Chapter 1

Autumn had painted the chestnut trees lining the quiet side street in the heart of Washington D.C.'s embassy district with brilliant color. The blazing reds and oranges and golds lent a festive, almost carnival air to the stately town houses shaded by their branches.

There was nothing festive in the air inside the town house midway down the block, however. A bronze plaque beside the door identified the building as home to the offices of the President's Special Envoy. Most Washington insiders knew the special envoy was one of those meaningless titles given by various administrations over the years to wealthy campaign contributors who wanted to rub elbows with the country's movers and shakers.

Only a handful of key presidential advisors knew the special envoy's real job. The incumbent also doubled as Director of OMEGA, an agency so secret its operatives were activated as a last resort, and then at the personal direction of the president.

One of those operatives was in the field now. And the shot he'd taken just moments ago had sent everyone in the high-tech control center on the third floor of the town house into a frenzy of activity.

Nick Jensen, code name Lightning, had served as OMEGA's director through three successive administrations. This one, he'd promised his wife and lively twins, would be his last. Until he walked out the door, however, he lived night and day with the knowledge that he put his agents' lives on the line every time he sent them into the field.

His eyes narrow and intent, Lightning studied the dual images projected onto the control center's wall-size screen. One was the face of the woman Wolf had captured in his crosshairs, digitized and transmitted back to OMEGA. The second image his people had pulled up after running the first through a highly sophisticated facial recognition program.

"Who is she?" he asked the tense operative standing next to him.

Deke Griffin, code name Ace, didn't hesitate. He'd acted as Wolf's controller from the start of this op, and he hadn't slept in almost forty-eight hours.

"Dr. Nina Nicole Grant," he replied, with no trace of his usual Texas twang. "Born Farmington, New Mexico. Graduated high school at sixteen. PhD in biology from University of New Mexico at twenty, followed three years later by an MBA from the same university."

A muscle ticked in the side of Lightning's jaw. "Smart woman."

"*Very* smart. She served as Director of Biomedical Research at Holbrook Laboratories. Left five years ago to start up Grant Medical Data Systems."

Ace paused, focusing intently on the left image. They'd pulled it from a *60 Minutes* segment on the latest crop of women to make the Fortune 500 list. The video still showed a slender businesswoman in a white blouse and neatly tailored black suit. Her light brown hair brushed her shoulders in a smooth, glossy sweep. Her caramel-colored eyes gazed at the camera with cool confidence.

"According to *60 Minutes*," he related tersely,

"Grant is well on her way to becoming one of the most successful entrepreneurs—male *or* female—under the age of thirty in this country."

"Smart and rich." The muscle in Lightning's jaw jumped again. "Just like DeWitt."

United States Senator Janice Dewitt, recently deceased. Victim or accomplice in a deadly, high-stakes game of espionage. It was OMEGA's job to find out which.

"What's Grant's connection to the target?"

"We haven't found one. We're still running her through the computers. If she and the target crossed paths anytime in the past, we'll smoke it out." Ace's eyes cut to the screen. "Maybe Wolf will have some luck on his end."

"He'd better," Lightning said, grimly. "We're fast running out of time. Tell him to make contact with Grant and nose out her game."

"Will do."

Ace flicked the switch on the console that put him in instant contact with Special Agent Rafe Blackstone, code name Wolf.

Wolf acknowledged Lightning's instructions, even as he kept the woman lined up in his scope. She'd lowered her oversize sunglasses just long enough for him to capture her image and transmit it instantly to OMEGA. The glasses were in place again, shielding her face, but he had her features imprinted on his brain. What he didn't have were answers to the questions her presence raised.

What the hell was she doing out here in the middle of nowhere? Alone. On foot. In the blazing sun. He tapped an impatient toe while a Hummer rattled down from the hacienda in answer to her call of a few moments ago.

"Paulo."

The figure stretched out beside Wolf cocked his head. "*Sí?*"

"Check the road from town. See if the woman has someone waiting for her."

With a nod, Special Agent Paulo Mendoza stuffed a pair of miniaturized but very high-powered binoculars into his shirt pocket and scuttled backward until he'd dropped below the line of sight of the hacienda's high-tech security cameras. Crouched low, he used the cover of prickly creosote and cactus to circle the base of the hill where he and Wolf had set up their surveillance. The only sound to mark his passage was a faint rattle of his boots on loose shale.

He returned mere moments later. "I spotted a car pulled over to the side of the road about a mile back. A rental, with the hood up."

Was it a ploy? A trick to gain entry to the heavily guarded hacienda? If so, it had worked. Wolf's stomach tightened as Grant climbed into the backseat of the dusty Hummer.

This had to be the rottenest vacation ever!

Forcing a smile, Nina declined her host's invitation to stay for tea on the tiled terrace overlooking the Sea of Cortez. She was hot and sweaty and in no mood for nice. Even with someone as urbane as the silver-maned expatriate whose men had just radioed in to say they'd reattached the fuel line that had shaken loose in Nina's rental.

"Thanks," she said with a smile, "but walking a mile in the sun took all the starch out of me. I'd better head back to town."

"Are you sure?" Sebastian Cordell's smile gleamed white against his deep tan. "It's not often such charming company is stranded almost at the gates of my hacienda."

"Some other time, perhaps."

"I shall hold you to that." Bowing, he kissed her hand with Old World graciousness. "My men will drive you to your car."

Nina winced as she traded the breeze-cooled shade of the portico for another blast of sun. With a nod to the muscled-up guard holding the Hummer's door, she climbed into the passenger seat.

Her escort's all-too-visible shoulder holster had sent her back a step when he'd first climbed out of his vehicle and asked her business. Tough Guy hadn't appeared the least bit sympathetic to her plight either. He'd checked inside her tote—for hidden weapons, she'd realized belatedly—then demanded to see some ID before he let her get anywhere close to the frigid air blasting from the Hummer interior. Sweat coursing between her breasts, Nina had handed over her wallet.

Not the smartest move, she admitted in retrospect, but this disaster was only the latest in a string of events that had thrown her off stride. The first was getting unengaged from the fiancé she'd discovered had tapped into her computer without her knowledge or consent and tried to milk the business connections she'd worked so hard to establish over the years. Connections that had helped transform her medical data digitization venture into a thriving enterprise with multimillion-dollar contracts.

You would think her employees would understand why she'd put her bruised heart into storage and devoted every waking hour to work. But no! Her entire staff, from her bossy executive assistant to the pimply adolescent who delivered the mail, had threatened to resign en masse if she didn't get out of the office and decompress, for God's sake!

So she *had* to fly down to Baja California. *Had* to check into an exclusive seaside resort. *Had* to twiddle her thumbs and force herself to vegetate by the pool for two days until a need to do something—anything—propelled her to jump in a rental car and drive out to view the remote seaside village her guidebook had touted as a "must see."

Then her rental car *had* to break down out there among the cactus and sun-baked hills. Where, she discovered, not a single bar popped up on her cell phone. Probably because she'd forgotten to charge the damn thing!

Thank God for the hacienda she'd spotted after a hot, dusty trek—and that the problem with her rental was so easily fixed. All she wanted now was a plunge in the pool at her resort, a frosty margarita, and some of that decompression time her staff insisted she needed.

Bracing herself for another blast of heat, Nina climbed out of the Hummer and thanked the two men who'd been sent to check the car. They sported shoulder holsters, too. Sebastian Cordell took his personal security seriously.

"Muchas gracias."

She fished a wad of pesos out of her straw tote, but the two men waved away the tip. Stuffing the pesos back in her bag, Nina thanked them again and slid behind the wheel. A dusty half hour later she hit the roundabout on the outskirts of Cabo San Lucas.

By then, a plunge in the pool had dropped well down her list of priorities. Her resort was another twenty minutes away. Her parched throat cried for something cold and wet—now! With that icy margarita in mind, she whipped the wheel and exited the roundabout. A screech of tires had her wincing and offering an apology to the vehicle that had pulled into the circle behind her.

"Sorry."

Luck was with her. She made only one wrong turn in Cabo's narrow streets before she found the multistory parking garage that served the inner harbor. The lower floors were full, but she zipped into an empty space on the fourth floor. Locking the rental car, she took the elevator down to the paved walkway leading to the marina.

According to her trusty guidebook, Cabo's protected inner harbor attracted sailboats and yachts from all over the world. A forest of tall silver masts validated that claim and acted as beacons to the restaurants, shops and bars lining the marina. Happy hour was in full swing Nina noted as she approached the crowded center. Lively salsa and mariachi music filled the air and souvenir hawkers had turned out en masse to capture the lucrative tourist trade.

She escaped most of the salesmen, but one particularly persistent youngster glued himself to her side. Flashing a grin, he flipped back a sleeve to display a skinny forearm banded with shiny bangles.

"*Hola, senorita!* You buy a bracelet from me, yes?"

"No, *gracias.*"

"These very good quality silver. From Taxco."

Right. Uh-huh. If those bangles were products of Mexico's fabled silver mines, she was Angelina Jolie.

"They're very nice," she replied diplomatically, "but I don't wear silver."

"Very good quality," he chorused again, twisting off a braided band. "Here, you try."

"No. *Gracias.* No."

"You try! You try!"

He grabbed her arm and shoved the braided band at her clenched fist. Half suspecting a ploy to distract her while one of his cohorts lifted her wallet from the tote slung over her shoulder, she tried to pull her arm back.

"No! I don't—"

"You heard the lady. Beat it, kid."

The deep growl spun both Nina and the pint-size vendor around. She looked up—not a common occurrence for someone who measured five eight in her bare feet—and felt her stomach do a flip.

Whoa, momma! Not two minutes ago, she'd been thinking of Angelina Jolie. Now here was James McAvoy, Angelina's sexy costar in *Wanted*. Same dark hair, same blue bedroom eyes, same chiseled chin.

Only this version was tougher. Leaner. Definitely not into Hollywood chic. His boots had collected almost as much dust as Nina's sandals. His wrinkled khaki trousers and the gaudy tropical shirt he wore over a black T-shirt, looked as though he'd just pulled them out of a suitcase. And the man needed a shave. Badly.

Nina was no stickler for protocol. Well, maybe a little. Okay, a lot. She expected her employees to present a neat, businesslike appearance at all times. That applied equally to everyone, from her division heads to the medical data-entry clerks.

She was fair about it, though. She held herself to the same strict standards. She dressed well, if conservatively, and worked out regularly to maintain both her health and her trim figure. She was conservative in her makeup, too. A few swipes of mascara was all she needed to enhance her brown eyes. Peach lip gloss did the trick for her mouth—which she now forced into a polite smile.

"Thanks for the assistance," she said as the kid who'd dogged her footsteps scampered away. "The boy was nothing, if not persistent."

"You have to learn how to shake 'em off. Must be your first time in Cabo."

It was a statement, not a question, but she answered it anyway. "Yes, it is."

Those blue eyes made a slow descent from her wide-brimmed straw hat to her designer sunglasses to the lips her ex-fiancé had described as all too kissable.

That was before she'd handed the conniving rat his walking papers, of course. During their last, somewhat less than cordial meeting, Kevin had flung other descriptive phrases at her. "Hard" and "stubborn" and "a real ball-buster" came immediately to mind.

"I was just going to have a beer." The dark-haired stranger hooked a thumb at the open-air bar behind him. "Care to join me?"

Thirst battled with common sense. If Nina hadn't been thinking of Kevin, odds were she would have turned down this casual invitation, just as she had that of the silver-maned hacienda owner. She *never* cruised bars, much less let strange men pick her up. But her parched throat and the remembered sting of Kevin's insults overcame caution.

"Sure. Why not?"

The Purple Parrot looked much like the dozens of other bars in the harbor area. Square tables topped by chipped formica crowded its railed-in veranda. Red and green-plastic chairs added a colorful air, as did the plastic pennants strung from corner to corner. Inside the bar itself were shelves lined with a staggering array of bottles.

"Over there."

Grasping Nina's elbow, the stranger steered her toward a just-vacated table with an unobstructed view of the marina. The sudden and totally unexpected sizzle that radiated up her bare arm flustered her so much she barely took in the sea of gleaming white sailboats.

"I'm Rafe," he said by way of introduction. "Rafe Blackstone."

"Nina. Uh, Grant."

Oh, for pity's sake! The heat must have gotten to her more than she'd realized. Bad enough she'd given in to the impulse to have a drink with a man who looked like a cross between a movie stud and a hood. One touch, and said stud came close to finishing what the sun had started. She was practically melting under her linen sundress.

It had to be that dark stubble on his cheeks and chin. Or the way his black T-shirt stretched across a taut, flat belly when he leaned back in his chair and unfolded his long legs. Or the slow, considering look he gave her through a screen of ridiculously thick lashes that any woman would have killed for.

Whatever it was, Nina responded in a way she'd never responded before to any male, Kevin included. A delicious spark of heat licked at her veins, and she could feel the muscles low in her belly tighten. Surprised and not a little flustered by her reaction, she removed her sunglasses and tipped the man seated across from her another polite smile.

"Where's home, Rafe?"

"Here and there. Mostly San Diego these days. You?"

"Albuquerque."

"What do you do there?"

Before she could answer, a waiter materialized

at their table. She ordered a margarita on the rocks, her companion a Dos Equis.

"I own and operate a company that digitizes medical data," she said when the waiter retreated.

"That so?" He arched a brow. "Given the president's push to computerize the medical profession, your business must be thriving."

"It is…now. We had some lean years when we first started out," she admitted wryly. "Hospitals weren't exactly anxious to share patient data. Plus, we had to make sure we didn't violate privacy laws. We got our foot in the door by trending data from local sources and providing it to medical facilities and research facilities across the state." A touch of pride crept into her voice. "We now harvest information from more than three thousand sources, analyze the input, and supply trends to a host of private and governmental medical research centers across the U.S."

"Only the U.S.?"

His slouch was the epitome of lazy relaxation, but his obvious interest reassured Nina. She always worried about boring folks with her passion for what she did. Or worse, lapsing into so much technical jargon that she lost her listeners completely.

"We still have to work within privacy laws," she said, "but I'm hoping to go international soon."

The seemingly casual comment put a sudden kink in Wolf's gut. The woman wanted to go international, did she? With the help of Sebastian Cordell, aka Stephen Caulder, aka a half-dozen other aliases?

Or was she after the sensitive, top-secret information Cordell had stolen and intended to auction to the highest bidder? Had she staged her vehicle's breakdown? Used it as an entree into Cordell's heavily guarded compound? Was she that good?

Wolf was still trying to decide when the waiter delivered their drinks. The man placed two frosted glasses in front of Grant and earned a surprised look.

"I didn't order two drinks."

"This is happy hour, señorita. You order one, I bring two."

"But…"

"Same price. No problem."

She gave in with a shrug and a smile.

Wolf had to give her credit. She had that polite half smile down pat. Friendly, but with just enough reserve in it to keep a man at a proper distance.

Nina Grant didn't know it yet, he thought grimly, but the two of them were about to get up close and *very* personal.

The muscles low in his belly tightened at the prospect. This is what he did. What he'd done now for almost ten years. Why he kept to himself and trusted no one outside his immediate circle of friends and fellow agents. Over the years, he'd locked horns with too many men and women who'd crossed the line. In more than one instance, it was kill or be killed.

In this one...

He didn't have a fix on Nina Grant yet, and the uncertainty scraped on his nerves. Extracting the lime wedge from the neck of his beer, he tipped the bottle in her direction.

"Here's to international cooperation."

She clinked her frosted glass against the bottle. "I'll drink to that."

He let the lager slide down his throat, watching while she licked some salt from the rim before taking a sip of her drink. The small act was completely natural, the way most people tasted a margarita—and disturbingly provocative. Wolf's belly tightened another notch as he followed the movement of her tongue.

Come on, he urged silently. *Drink the damn thing.*

He knew from experience that two-for-one happy hour drinks at most Cabo San Lucas dives were usually so watered down you couldn't even taste the booze in them. The Purple Parrot, however, had a reputation to maintain. That's why he'd chosen it. Another double round, and he'd have Nina Grant singing like a tanked-up canary.

"How long have you lived in Albuquerque?" he asked to get the ball rolling.

"I got a job there after grad school and decided to stay. I love the climate. The people. The mountains. The incredible sunsets. Seems I've spent almost as much time traveling recently as I have at home, though. I almost cringe when I have to get on a plane these days."

Wolf pumped her for information, subtly, smoothly, and hid a smile of satisfaction when she took another taste of her drink.

"Whew! This is potent."

"Not that potent. It goes down easier after the first few sips."

"I'll bet." Her nose wrinkling, she set the glass aside. "It's hitting my empty stomach like a sledgehammer. I'd better stop with this one and head to my hotel."

So much for his plan to get her sloshed. No matter. He wasn't about to let her wiggle out of his net now.

"So let me buy you dinner."

Chapter 2

Nina blinked at Blackstone's unexpected invitation. An automatic refusal formed on her lips. Before she could voice it, his cell phone emitted a low, vibrating hum.

"'Scuse me." He slipped a sleek little jobbie out of his pocket and held it at an angle. "Sorry, I need to read this text message."

"No problem."

His face remained impassive as he scrolled the screen. She couldn't tell if the news was good or bad, but the brief interruption gave Nina time to reconsider his surprising offer of dinner.

She had to admit it was tempting. *Extremely*

tempting. She didn't need her string of degrees—or the intent look in this sexy stranger's eyes—to make the leap from drinks to dinner to a quick tumble into bed.

The mere thought made her throat go tight. It affected other parts of her, too. Parts that hadn't felt this sudden sizzle in way too long.

No surprise there. She was a biologist by training and a medical researcher by profession. She knew she possessed a normal, healthy sex drive. One that she and Kevin had made the most of. At first.

In the later stages of their engagement, their lovemaking had been less adventurous. It went decidedly flat when she began to suspect he'd courted her more for what she could do for him in the business arena than in the bedroom.

Maybe... Maybe this was just what she needed. An hour or two or three of hot, sweaty, completely mindless sex. What better way to get over the humiliation of Kevin's lies? How better to revalidate herself as a woman?

Ha! Who was she kidding? Inviting Blackstone back to her hotel had nothing whatsoever to do with validation, and a *whole* lot to do with his impact on her pulmonary system. The mere thought of peeling off his T-shirt and popping the snap on those wrinkled khaki's constricted her lungs and put a lump the size of Rhode Island in her throat.

Unfortunately, the biologist in her didn't have to delve very deep to compile a comprehensive list of diseases she could pick up by exchanging bodily fluids with a total stranger. Even one as hot as Rafe Blackstone. *Especially* one as hot as Blackstone. With a stab of real regret, she groped for the tote bag hooked over the back of her chair.

"Thanks, but I'll pass on dinner, too. Let me pay for the drinks."

"I'll get them."

"Really, I want to. I've enjoyed our—"

"I've got it covered."

Oooh-kay. She dropped her wallet back into her tote. That was twice today she'd stepped on it: first with the guys who'd fixed the fuel line on her rental, now with Blackstone. Guess she shouldn't have let his bristles and rumpled shirt mislead her into thinking he would appreciate a woman who preferred to pay her own way.

"I'll walk you to your car."

She started to decline the offer. The vendors milling outside the bar, waiting to pounce, changed her mind. With the sun gone down and the crowds of tourists thinning out, they would swarm all over her. Why not let this lean, tough-looking gringo deal with them?

Which he did, with a few well-chosen words. He also took her arm to weave a path for her through the grumbling souvenir hawkers. His hold was loose but oddly possessive. To Nina's consternation, the feel of his callused palm raised goose bumps over every exposed inch of skin.

She covered her involuntary reaction with a nod toward the rapidly darkening sky. "Cools off fast when the sun goes down, doesn't it?"

"It does," he replied, and promptly tucked her closer into his side.

His scent enveloped her. The seductive blend of sun-warmed skin and healthy male sweat retriggered the erotic sensations Nina was so determined to repress. Gulping, she tried to focus on the dramatic red-and-gold streaks in the dark sky, the raucous beat of music coming from the restaurants, anything but the man beside her.

She failed miserably and breathed a distinct sigh of relief when they reached the parking garage. Easing free of his hold, she punched the button for the fourth floor.

"Thanks again for the drinks."

"I'll ride up with you."

She turned to him with a polite but firm no

on her lips. He spiked it with a shrug and casual remark.

"This part of town is usually pretty safe, but a couple of tourists were mugged in this garage a few days ago."

Common sense prevailed. Parking garages in any part of the world could be risky. No sense tempting fate.

Which was exactly what she was doing by prolonging her brief association with Blackstone. She wasn't fooling anyone, herself included. The tingling awareness of his proximity, the delicious feeling of temptation rode all the way up to the fourth floor with her.

They stepped out into cavernous gloom. Their footsteps echoed as Nina led the way up the ramp, glad now that she'd accepted Blackstone's escort. The garage had emptied considerably since her arrival. Probably because most of the businesses in town that didn't cater exclusively to the tourist trade had closed for the day. Her rental now sat by itself at the end of the row.

Digging the keys out of her tote, she clicked the remote. The lights flashed, the locks popped, and she turned to her escort once more. He was close. A little too close. She put on a cool smile.

"Thanks again. I enjoyed—"

"Let me have the keys."

"Excuse me?"

"Give me the keys. I'll drive you back to your hotel."

Okay, enough is enough. Lifting her chin, Nina shook her head.

"Look, I don't know what signals you think I sent there at the bar, but you read them wrong."

"Give me the keys."

When he took a step closer, crowding her against the car, fright exploded in her chest. How stupid was this? How stupid was *she?*

She threw a wild glance down the ramp. Nothing moved. Not a single person walked to or from a car. No headlights stabbed through the gloom. She was on her own here.

Her throat clogged with fear, she tried to recall any of the moves from the self-defense courses she'd taken over the years. All she could remember, all she could think of was to yell her head off and gouge her attacker's eyes with her car keys.

She fumbled the pointed ends between her fingers, balled her fist, and screamed for help. Or tried to. She didn't emit much more than a squeak before Blackwater clapped a hard hand over her mouth. His other hand batted away the arm she'd brought up in a vicious arc.

She fought him, using every bit of her strength, but he was too big, too strong. Reaching behind her, he ripped open the car door and shoved her inside.

Her heart hammering in terror, Nina landed in a sprawl across the driver's seat. Pure instinct brought her knee up and her foot lashing out. Blackstone dodged the kick aimed at his groin, and took it on the outside of his thigh instead.

"Calm down!" he got out with a grunt of pain. "I'm not going to hurt you."

Right. Uh-huh. Sure.

She wasn't about to take his word for it. With his unyielding presence blocking the exit, she scrambled over the center console and made a desperate lunge for the passenger door. Cursing, he dropped into the driver's seat and wrapped fingers of steel around her upper arm. A swift yank jerked her back down.

"Listen to me. I'm not going to hurt you."

"Then let me go!"

"Not yet. And not here." He kept her in place with an iron fist. "We need to talk, Dr. Grant."

Dr. Grant?

The title penetrated her wild fear. She hadn't used the honorific in conversation. She was sure she hadn't. She rarely did, and then only in professional circles. So how did he know?

"Who are you?" she panted. "What do you want to talk to me about?"

"I'll tell you at the Mayan Princess."

Oh, Lord! He knew where she was staying. Had he followed her from the resort? Been following her the entire day?

He couldn't have! She would have spotted him out on that winding, dusty road before her rental broke down.

If it *had* broken down. What if he'd sabotaged her car? Anticipated that she'd be stranded out there in the middle of nowhere? Which she would have been, if she hadn't trudged a mile through the hot sun to Sebastian Cordell's hacienda. Or was that part of his diabolical plan, too?

The questions hammered at her as he eased his brutal grip, but she decided not to stick around for the answers. She made another grab for the door handle, only to hear the door locks snick.

"Child protective locks," he commented laconically as she tugged futilely on the handle.

Grinding her teeth in frustration, she sank back against the seat. Her cell phone was in her tote, she remembered. With a dead battery. Her last hope she thought as her abductor keyed the ignition, was the garage attendant.

Except there wasn't one. The booth where she'd forked over a fee when she'd entered was now empty. Apparently, anyone who drove in after the main businesses and shops closed got to park free.

Nor was there a police officer anywhere in sight when they pulled out of the garage and hit the streets. Nina seriously considered hammering on the window to attract the attention of the people out for a late evening stroll. A return of her common sense—and gradual subsiding of panic—subdued the impulse.

Blackstone said he didn't intend to hurt her. He also said he'd tell her what he wanted from her at the Mayan. That meant he had to pull up at the entrance to the posh resort, where the extremely well-trained parking valet, doorman and desk clerks all knew her by name. Blackstone could hardly waltz into the resort with her and waltz out again, leaving behind her dead and/or mutilated body and a small army of people who could ID him.

Could he?

She'd more or less reassured herself on that point by the time the resort appeared in the distance.

She'd also worked up as much reluctant curiosity as distrust. What the heck did this man want with her? She was pretty sure now it wasn't sex, and was shocked by the contradictory feelings that realization generated.

"Turn here," she muttered as they approached the long, winding drive that led up to the resort. When he flipped on the directionals, the lingering remnants of Nina's fear eased. He really *was* taking her back to the Mayan. She let out a low sigh of relief.

The resort was the latest in a string of San Cabo resorts that included Westin and Ritz Carlton and other high-priced escapes. Constructed to resemble a Mayan temple, the main building sat on a cliff overlooking the sea. Tall palms lined the drive leading up to it. Lit by floodlights, they provided an exotic approach to the stunningly dramatic pyramid gleaming against the night sky.

As Nina had anticipated, a valet came forward when the car rolled to a stop. He had to wait for Blackstone to hit the lock release to open her door. When he did, she scrambled out with considerably more haste than dignity.

"*Buenas tardes,* Dr. Grant. Did you have a good drive this afternoon?"

"I've had better, Ramon." Determined to

establish a record of events, Nina pointed to the driver rounding the front end of the car. "This is Señor Blackstone. Rafe Blackstone. He's visiting me. For a *short* time."

Ramon took the hint. "*Buenas tardes,* Señor. Will you need this car when you leave? If so, I will park it here by the entrance instead of taking it down to the lot."

"Here's good." Blackstone slipped him a folded bill with the car keys and took Nina's elbow. "Lead the way."

She did, making sure to repeat his name to the doorman and the clerks on duty in the breezeway that served as a reception area.

"There's a waiter over there by the pool," Blackstone drawled. "You want to introduce me to him, too?"

"You think this is funny?" she huffed. "Somehow, I don't find kidnapping amusing. Neither, I suspect, would the local police."

"Police down in these parts take a different view of things, but you can call them if you want. Ask for Chief Inspector Mannie Diaz. Tell him you're with me."

"Well, for…!"

Thoroughly indignant, Nina came to a dead stop. Hands on hips, she faced her tormentor.

"Why didn't you tell me you're a cop back there in town instead of scaring the crap out of me?"

"I'm not a cop."

"Oh. Well." That set her back a bit, but she recovered quickly. "So what are you?"

"We'll talk about that in your suite. Where is it?"

"You don't know?" she said snidely. "You seem to know everything else."

Ignoring the comment, he urged her through the open-air lobby to the pool beyond. It was one of four at the resort. Two catered to families, the other two to adults only. The one on this level was an infinity pool, its floodlit waters seeming to flow over the edge and drop straight into the sea far below.

Instead of booking her into the main hotel, Nina's superefficient assistant had reserved one of the casitas that clung to the cliffs behind the pyramid. They were quieter and more private—qualities Nina had very much appreciated until this moment.

Some of her nervousness returned as she led the way down several flights of steps and around bougainvillea-draped walls. The only sounds to disturb the evening quiet were the soft music emanating from hidden speakers along the walkways and the ever-present murmur of the sea.

By the time she'd reached her casita, however, her indignation had returned. Along with it came a healthy bout of anger. Fishing her key card out of her tote, she unlocked the door and marched inside. The spacious, beautifully decorated unit featured tile floors, a fully equipped kitchen, one bedroom with a master bath to die for and a small Jacuzzi tucked in a corner of the balcony that was suspended over the sea.

Nina didn't give her uninvited guest time to admire the ambience. Flinging her tote on a sofa covered in muted jungle print, she folded her arms across her chest.

"All right, Blackstone. If that's really your name. What's this all about?"

"It's really my name," he confirmed, glancing around. When those laser blue eyes came back to Nina, they sliced into her like a scalpel. "And this is about your friend, Sebastian Cordell."

"Huh?"

Of all the things she'd expected… Okay, she hadn't known *what* to expect. But this certainly wasn't it.

"Are you talking about the older gentleman I met this afternoon?"

"I'm talking about the man who invited you into his hacienda this afternoon." His jaw hardened. "As for whether or not he's a gentleman, you tell me."

This was getting way too bizarre. Frowning, Nina tapped a foot. "Before I tell you anything, *I* want some answers. Who are you and who do you work for?"

"I told you my name. Most of the time I run a marine construction company."

"Other times?"

"I do independent consulting. Hazard elimination. Debris removal. That sort of thing."

The sideline seemed legitimate. It was just the way he said it. As though there was more to removing debris than hauling it off in dump trucks or barges.

Nina's foot tapped again. "I want to see some ID."

With a sardonic shrug, he extracted a well-worn leather wallet from his back pocket and flipped it open to a California driver's license.

There he was. Rafael Conall Blackstone. Height, 6'2". Hair: black. Eyes: Blue. Weight: a really buff 180.

" 'Conall'?"

"My grandmother's Irish." A gleam flickered in

his eyes, quickly come and just as quickly gone. "It translates to 'strong wolf'."

For some reason, the fact that he had a grandmother made him seem more human. Less dangerous. Which she knew was really absurd. Like murderers and rapists didn't?

"My turn." He slid the wallet back into his pocket. "What were..."

"Not so fast, Blackstone. I'm not finished yet."

Impatience rippled across his face. Making an obvious effort to contain it, he hooked one of the high stools from the marble counter separating the kitchen from the dining area and swung it around.

Nina gave a huff of disgust. "Make yourself comfortable, why don't you?"

He did, with one long leg braced against the floor tiles and the other propped on the stool's rung. "What else do you want to ask me?"

"Oh, just a few little things. Like how you knew I hold a PhD. And where I'm staying. And that I met Sebastian Cordell this afternoon. Oh, yes—one more. There's also the question of why in hell you didn't ask me about this guy in town instead of kidnapping and scaring the crap out of me!"

He had the grace to look a little ashamed. Not

much. Just enough to suggest he didn't go around abducting women every day of the week.

"Yeah, well, I'm sorry about that. To tell the truth, I planned to pour a couple more margaritas down you, get you loose, and pump you for information there at the Purple Parrot. When that didn't work, you forced me to resort to more direct measures."

"*What* information?"

"For starters, how you know Cordell."

"I don't know him! Or I didn't, before my car broke down this afternoon."

"Pretty convenient, how you arranged for it to break down so close to his compound."

"'Convenient'?" Nina echoed, incredulously. "'Arranged'?"

Thoroughly flummoxed, she groped for the other bar stool and yanked it closer so she could plop down. This whole thing was becoming more absurd by the moment.

"Why would I 'arrange' a breakdown?"

The rueful note disappeared from his voice. Hard and sharp-edged, it cut through the air between them.

"Maybe because Sebastian Cordell has something to sell. Something you might want," he added, his eyes locked on hers. "You and a number of other *entrepreneurs*."

The small sneer accompanying the last word brought Nina's chin up with a snap. She'd worked damn hard to establish her company. She'd sunk every penny of her savings into start-up costs, then borrowed heavily to purchase the building Grant Medical Data Systems now operated out of. The first months—the first years—had been scary as hell.

But she'd pulled it off. By sheer luck and perfect timing, she'd gotten in on the ground floor of a burgeoning and very necessary industry, and now turned an extremely healthy profit. One no one could sneer at!

Bristling, she poked a finger at Blackstone's chest. "You listen to me, fella. I'm going to say this one time and one time only. I did not arrange to have my car break down. I did not use it as a ploy to meet Sebastian Cordell. And I am *not* interested in whatever the man has for sale."

"Then why…"

The shrill ring of the phone sitting at the end of the counter cut him off.

"That," Nina announced, with fierce satisfaction, "is most likely Ramon, checking to see if he should move the car to the parking lot. I'll tell him to call you a taxi."

"Not yet."

"Yes, yet! This conversation is over." Glaring at him, she snatched up the receiver. *"Hola."*

The smooth, cultured voice that came through the earpiece made her swallow. Hard. With a helpless look in Blackstone's direction, she responded to the gracious inquiry.

"Yes, Mr. Cordell, I made it home safely."

Every muscle in Blackstone's body went taut. His narrowed gaze drilled into Nina as she clutched the receiver.

"What? Lunch tomorrow at your hacienda? I... Uh..."

Chapter 3

Wolf's gut twisted. Cordell! The prey he'd been sent to take down. The same bastard suspected of extracting top secret information from a United States senator. Now oozing his poisonous charm into Nina Grant's ear.

And here Wolf had come so close to believing the woman. Almost swallowed her tale of a breakdown. Damn near let her air of righteous indignation and melting, brown-sugar eyes convince him she'd flown down to Cabo on vacation as she claimed.

Yet...

The terse message Ace had texted a little while ago indicated they'd come up empty at their end.

OMEGA could access a host of databases, public, private and otherwise. Wolf knew damn well they'd run Nina Grant through every one. Yet none of the agency's wizards had been able to turn up a connection between Grant and Sebastian Cordell. As far as they could tell, she was clean.

Until this moment, everything in Wolf concurred with that assessment. He'd lived on the razor's edge so long he'd learned to trust his instincts where people were concerned. The short time he'd spent with her had him ninety-nine-percent convinced Nina Grant was the busy exec on vacation she claimed to be. The finger she'd poked in his chest moments ago had just about clinched the matter in his mind.

He had only a second to decide whether to go with his gut-level assessment. A mere heartbeat, while she looked at him, wide-eyed and stuttering, to come up with an answer to Cordell's invitation.

"Yes," Wolf hissed. "Tell him yes!"

He could see the doubt in her face, the distrust. Her knuckles were white on the receiver, her body taut with indecision. He was sure she would refuse his urgent request when she cleared her throat.

"Lunch sounds delightful, Mr. Cordell." Her eyes remained locked on Wolf's. "Twelve-thirty it is. No, no need to send someone to pick me up. I'll drive myself. What? Oh. Right. I guess I do need your phone number in case I get lost or stranded again. Let me get a pen."

Wolf had Cordell's numbers. All of them. But he kept silent while she hunted down a pencil and jotted a string of digits on a paper napkin.

"I've got it. Thanks. I'll...I'll see you tomorrow."

He was in! Or she was. Wolf contained his fierce elation as she hung up the receiver and stared at it blankly for a few seconds.

"I can't believe I just did that." Her eyes lifted to his. "*Why* did I just do that?"

"I can't speak to the why," he said slowly, "but I'll tell you this. A whole bunch of folks will be real happy that you did."

"At the risk of repeating myself...why?"

He sifted the details in his mind, sorting out what he could and couldn't tell her, and decided on the varying shades of the truth.

"I told you I freelance on occasion."

"Right." Her forehead crinkling, she repeated the line he'd given her. "At which time you specialize in eliminating hazards and removing debris."

"One of those hazards is Sebastian Cordell."

"Aha!"

Despite the seriousness of the situation, a grin

tugged at the corners of Wolf's mouth. "Aha"? Who said "aha" these days, outside of a slapstick comedy? Dr. Nina Grant, apparently.

She looked indignant again, like a tabby cat who'd been about to pounce and got its whiskers pulled instead.

"So that story about being into marine construction was just that?" she huffed. "A story?"

"No, that part's true. I do this as a sideline."

"Some sideline!" Frowning, she chewed on her lower lip for a few moments. "So why do you consider Sebastian Cordell a hazard?"

"We suspect he courted and seduced the senior senator from Maine."

"Janice DeWitt?" she gasped. "The senator who died in a car accident a few weeks ago?"

"There's some question," Wolf said carefully, "whether it was an accident or a suicide." Or something else.

So far the FBI and Secret Service had managed to suppress the evidence indicating that a member of the U.S. Congress had deliberately driven her vehicle through a guardrail and over a rocky cliff. Likewise the gut-wrenching e-mail she'd sent the President Pro Tem of the Senate, confessing that a disk encrypted with highly classified information might have been compromised by the man she'd taken as a lover.

"We also suspect," Wolf continued soberly, "Cordell may have used the senator to gain access to extremely sensitive top secret information."

Nina took a step back, and her shock that a popular, charismatic senator had indulged in an extramarital affair and possibly committed suicide took an instant and very personal turn. The information Kevin had downloaded from her personal computer certainly wasn't top secret, but it *had* been crucial to her business. She would have shared it with him if he'd asked. Not all of it, of course, just the nonproprietary data that might have been useful to his financial planning and investment operation. That he'd dug into her private files without her knowledge or consent had stunned her. That he'd leveraged the data he'd extracted to benefit one of her competitors had royally pissed her off.

"Bastard," she muttered.

"Yeah, he is."

Pulled back to the present, she blinked. "I was referring to the jerk who pulled almost the same thing on me."

Blackstone cocked his head. "How so?"

It embarrassed her to admit how blind she'd

been. She had to force herself to recap the sorry details.

"My fiancé stole proprietary information and sold it to a competitor. Correction, make that ex-fiancé."

She wasn't looking for sympathy. Good thing, because the man seated on the bar stool a few feet from her didn't display so much as a trace of it. Instead, a gleam of satisfaction leapt into his blue eyes.

"Then you understand why we're so anxious to nail Sebastian Cordell."

"I understand it," Nina replied cautiously, "but I don't see how my having lunch with him will help."

"We've been trying to get someone inside the compound. Unfortunately, Cordell's goon squad take their duties very seriously."

"I noticed."

"But Cordell just issued you an engraved invitation. We can fit you with a hidden camera, have you—"

"Whoa! Hold on there, Blackstone."

With the shoulder holsters strapped onto the goons he'd just mentioned all too vivid in her mind, Nina scrambled off her stool and backed away.

"I'm not into playing spy games."

"This isn't a game," he fired back.

"Yes, well, whatever it is, I'll leave it to the pros like you."

Blackstone vacated his stool and followed her into the living area. Like the rest of the casita, the room was elegantly furnished. A three-section sofa in muted colors formed a conversation pit, with a monster slab of white-veined black marble in the middle to serve as a coffee table. Facing the sofas was an entertainment center containing a sixty-inch flat screen TV, a DVD player, an assortment of recent movies and an iPod dock.

Nina's iPod and earbuds were still in her straw tote, so the only sound in the room, as she faced Blackstone was the restless murmur of the sea below the balcony, just off the living area.

"We need your cooperation, Dr. Grant. Cordell plans to auction the information he stole to the highest bidder. If it falls into the wrong hands—an unfriendly government or a terrorist organization, for instance—it could seriously jeopardize U.S. national security."

"Oh, sure. Lay the safety and security of the United States on my shoulders, why don't you?"

Nervously, Nina swiped her palms down the side seams of her linen sundress. She'd always considered herself a good citizen. She paid her taxes on time, donated to a number of charities, gave blood regularly and volunteered at a homeless shelter one weekend a month.

She did not, however, in any way, shape or form, see herself as a modern day Mata Hari. The prospect of entering Sebastian Cordell's heavily guarded compound with a camera hidden somewhere on her person made her break out in a cold sweat.

"Look, Blackstone, I'd like to help. I really would. This just isn't my area of expertise."

"We have from now until tomorrow noon. I'll make sure you know what you're doing before you go in."

Her palms froze in midswipe. "From now until tomorrow noon?" she echoed. "What are you planning to do? Camp out here tonight?"

"If that's what it will take to make you comfortable with the operation."

If anything, the prospect of spending the next twelve-plus hours in close quarters with Rafe Blackstone made her twice as nervous.

"It won't work," she told him firmly. "I'm the world's worst liar. Even a little social fib makes my face turn red, and I can't look people in the eye."

"Must be tough to conduct business negotiations," he drawled.

"Not particularly," she snapped, her chin coming up. "I conduct negotiations fairly and honestly."

The icy reply knifed through the air like a blade. Blackstone dipped his head in acknowledgment of the hit and hooked his thumbs in the pockets of his wrinkled khakis. The movement swung open the flaps of his jungle print shirt and gave Nina an unobstructed view of black cotton stretched across a muscled chest, but she was too miffed to appreciate the view.

"About those negotiations," he said, with a considering look. "Didn't you tell me earlier that your company supplies medical trend data to a host of private and governmental research centers?"

"Yes. So?"

"So I'm guessing government contracts must account for a sizable chunk of your business."

Nina drew in a swift breath. Government contracts accounted for more than a chunk. They constituted almost half of her business base.

"You'd better not be thinking what I think you're thinking, Blackstone!"

"If you're thinking those contracts can be cancelled with one phone call, I guess I am."

He didn't so much as blink. The bald-faced effrontery of it, the sheer gall, made Nina gasp.

"I don't believe this! You're actually trying to blackmail me into helping you?"

"Not trying, Dr. Grant."

He was dead serious. She could see it in his eyes, in the set of his jaw. She open her mouth to tell him go straight to hell. Then she remembered how many people she had on her payroll and snapped it shut again.

She'd worked so hard to build her business. Everyone at Grant Medical Systems had. Without their government contracts, she would have to cut back. Lay off a dozen or more employees. Grinding her teeth, she yielded.

"All right. I'll scout out Cordell's compound for you. Just so you know, though, he and my sleaze of an ex-fiancé aren't the only bastards I've encountered lately."

Wolf hid a wince. Exploiting snitches and useful contacts were part of *his* business. He'd never hesitated to strong-arm anyone into cooperating before. He wouldn't hesitate in the future. That didn't lessen the bite from the scorn in Nina Grant's brown eyes—or explain why it bothered him so much.

"I need to contact my people and have them send the equipment."

She waved a hand toward the phone on the

counter and treated him to a caustic smile. "Be my guest."

"I'll use my own."

He slid back the balcony doors and went outside. The triangular hot tub tucked into a corner of the deck drew a wry smile. Not a good spot for the acrophobic, suspended over the sea the way it was. But the bubbling water and the waves pounding against the rocky shore below provided an excellent sound buffer for a private conversation.

As he had at the Purple Parrot, Wolf angled the instrument so its built-in iris scanner instantly identified him. One click of a key connected him to OMEGA control. Ace's unshaven face filled the screen.

"What's happening, pardner?"

"A new development." His glance cut to the woman standing rigid with anger in the center of the living room. "Dr. Grant's having lunch at Cordell's hacienda tomorrow."

"Damn! We scrubbed her, Wolf. Up one side and down the other. We couldn't find a connection."

"She swears there isn't one, other than the chance meeting this afternoon."

"So what's with lunch?"

"I suspect Cordell researched her, too. As

we both know, the man has a taste for wealthy, attractive women."

His glance raked Nina Grant from head to foot. Attractive didn't really describe the doc. She wasn't what Hollywood types would label a classic beauty. Her chin was too stubborn and her mouth lacked the collagen pout that seemed to be the standard these day. Especially now, when she'd folded her lips into a tight, angry line and her eyes shot daggers at the man who'd invaded her luxury casita.

She had one hell of a body, though. Long and well toned and curved in all the right places. When he'd followed her along the pathway to the marina, Wolf had caught more than enough of her silhouette backlighted through her linen dress to know he'd give her his vote anytime, any place.

Ace's low whistle jerked his attention away from Nina Grant and back to the business at hand. "You think Cordell is planning to hit on her, the way he did DeWitt?"

"I think it's a distinct possibility."

"Does she know that?"

"No, but I'll make sure she does before she joins him for lunch tomorrow."

Ace lifted a brow. "She's cooperating with us?"

"She is, although she's not real happy about it."

Guilt bit at Wolf again as he explained about the government contracts. "I want her rigged out before she goes in, Ace. Tell Mac we need the best she's got in her bag of tricks."

"Will do."

Mackenzie Blair had served as guru of all things electronic for OMEGA and several other highly specialized government agencies until the birth of her twins. She was now on an extended leave of absence but still provided her expertise to OMEGA on request. Not surprising, since she was married to Nick Jensen.

"I'll take care of it," Ace promised. "You should have a delivery within the next couple hours."

"Have them deliver it to the Mayan Princess. Dr. Grant's casita."

"Roger that. And I'll update Lightning when I contact Mac."

"Thanks."

Flipping the phone shut, Rafe went back inside.

"Okay," he told the woman standing with her back stiff and her arms crossed, regarding him with all the warmth she would one of Mexico's spiny iguanas. "I've got some equipment on the way. It should be here in a few hours."

"What kind of equipment?"

"A special camera. It will be so small you won't even know you're wearing it. You can…"

"Good God!" Her arms dropped. "You were really serious? You want to rig me out with spy gadgets?"

"We'll rig you out with more than a gadget. The woman responsible for our electronic surveillance devices is the best in the business."

And diabolically clever. Mackenzie Blair had sent agents into the field equipped with everything from invisible skin patches with embedded satellite communication capability, to a translucent jade pendant that emitted silent and completely disabling ultrahigh-frequency sound waves.

"Count on whatever device she sends being completely invisible to the untrained eye," Wolf assured his extremely reluctant recruit.

"Untrained being the operative word."

Grant shook her head stubbornly, her soft brown hair swirling around her face.

"Cordell's goons, as you call them, almost did a strip search before they let me through the gate this afternoon. What if they do the same tomorrow?"

"Trust me, they won't detect whatever we equip you with."

"*Trust* you?" Scorn dripped from every word. "You expect me to trust a man who scares me half to death, then blackmails me into cooperating with him?"

Wolf bit back a sigh. He could tell it was going to be a long night.

"Sit down, Dr. Grant. I'll talk you through exactly what I want you to do, step by step."

As promised, Ace briefed Lightning when he contacted him and Mac at home that evening. He briefed the boss again at 11:00 a.m. DC time the next morning, following a terse update from Wolf.

After checking the status board to confirm Lightning was in his office, Ace took the titanium-shielded elevator that zipped individuals from the control center to the offices of the special envoy on the first floor. Before exiting, he checked the security screen displaying the entire first-floor reception area. Although Lightning's executive assistant had cleared him to see the boss, Chelsea Jackson was relatively new to OMEGA operations. She'd replaced silver-haired Elizabeth Wells, who'd retired a few months ago and waltzed off into the sunset with the orthopedic surgeon who'd done her hip replacement.

Jackson was brisk and efficient, but a number of OMEGA operatives—Ace included—had yet to warm up to her. Maybe because she *was* so brisk and efficient. In contrast to grandmotherly Elizabeth, Ms. Jackson kept her personal life private and maintained a polite but firm distance from the field agents.

The shield was in place when she greeted Ace. "I informed Lightning you were on your way down," she said in her cool, Boston brahman voice. "Go right in."

Ace stifled the impulse to linger beside her Louis XV desk and coax a smile out of the woman. What he had for Lightning was too urgent. He couldn't resist revving up his Texas twang, however.

"Thanks, darlin'."

She did her best to hide a flicker of annoyance while she pressed the hidden button that gave him access to Lightning's private office. Ace caught it though, and allowed himself a brief grin before he entered the inner sanctum.

As befitted the President's Special Envoy, the office contained enough polished mahogany to panel a medium-size castle. Bypassing the conference table that took up a good portion of the room, Ace took one of the high-backed chairs set in front of Lightning's desk.

"I just briefed the president an hour ago on our plan to infiltrate Cordell's compound," OMEGA's tawny-haired director said. "I hope you're not going to tell me there's been a change of direction."

"Sorry, Chief. There has."

Sighing, Nick loosened the knot of his red silk tie. He'd held this job long enough to know nothing ever went down as originally orchestrated. Given the stakes in this op, however, he'd hoped for the best.

"What's the glitch?"

"Dr. Grant."

"She's changed her mind about cooperating?" he asked, sharply.

"She hasn't changed her mind. Wolf has. He says Grant doesn't have the makings of an undercover operative. The mere prospect of going in wired gets her all nervous and flustered. If we send her in alone, he's convinced she'll tip Cordell we're on to him."

"Damn it!" Blowing out a frustrated breath, Lightning thrust a hand through his sun-streaked hair. "She was our best bet for getting inside the compound."

"She still is, but Wolf is going with her."

"How?"

"Turns out Grant recently dumped her fiancé." A wry grin creased Ace's bristly, unshaven cheeks. "Wolf intends to step into his shoes."

Chapter 4

"You're crazy! All of you!"

Completely wrung out by her long, frustrating night, Nina glared at the three men facing her across the coffee table. Cups ringed with the dregs of the countless pots of coffee they'd consumed were scattered on the polished slab of marble, as were the remnants of the breakfast her uninvited guests had ordered from room service.

"It's the only way, Dr. Grant."

That came from Chief Inspector Manuel Diaz. Sad-eyed and scarecrow thin, Diaz and one of his henchmen had rapped on the door to Nina's casita well past midnight. They'd brought with them an almost microscopic wireless device hidden inside a pearl button. Flown in by jet at the request of El Lobo, Diaz had advised her.

El Lobo. The Wolf. Otherwise known as Rafe Blackstone. If that was really his name. Nina wouldn't put it past him to have faked that California driver's license.

He stood across from her now, hands on hips and his face set with a frustration to match hers. Tough! It wasn't her fault she couldn't work the damn camera. She'd *told* this guy, Wolf, she was a terrible liar. Although he and Mannie Diaz had done their best to coax her out of her jitters, she'd fumbled every attempt to appear nonchalant while scanning the interior of her own casita. So how the heck was she supposed to pull off scanning Cordell's entire hacienda, much less hide the listening device they wanted her to plant.

She'd finally given up around 4:00 a.m., and announced she was going to take a break while they figured out an alternate solution. They'd waited to drop that solution on her until late midmorning, after she'd finished a late breakfast of bacon and eggs scrambled with salsa, delivered by room service.

"If I can't carry off a hidden scanner," she threw at the three men lined up like a firing squad, "how in God's name do you expect me to carry off a pretend fiancé?"

Sad-eyed Mannie Diaz replied for all three. "This man, this Kevin James, he breaks your heart, yes?"

Actually, a few weeks of time and distance had made Nina realize Kevin the Jerk had hurt her pride more than her heart. She wasn't about to admit that to these three characters, however.

"Now this *estúpido* appears without warning here in Cabo San Lucas," Mannie continued. "He tells you he's sorry. He pleads with you to take him back. Of course you are upset and very confused. But you have accepted Cordell's invitation to lunch. It would be most impolite to back out now. So you call him, yes? You ask him—no, you *tell* him you have a guest you wish to bring with you."

"It won't work," she insisted, with a glare in Señor Wolf's direction. "You don't know anything about me. Where I went to high school. What kind of music I like."

"Farmington Regional High School," he fired back. "Mostly jazz and easy rock, with a hefty dose of show tunes thrown in for flavoring."

When Nina gaped at him, he gestured to the iPod sitting in the dock in the entertainment center.

"The music part was easy. And you left your tote

on the counter," he said without a trace of apology. "Between that and the information the people at my headquarters dug up on you, I know more than enough to play your very contrite lover."

"It won't work," she repeated, with a touch of desperation. "You may have gleaned a few facts about me, but I know nothing about you."

"I'll tell you all you need to know during the drive out to Cordell's place. At the same time, you can tell me about this guy you were engaged to. Pick up the phone, Nina. Call Cordell. Remember, this lunch is as much in your interest as ours."

"You," she got out through clenched teeth, "are really despicable."

He shrugged aside the insult with the same ease he'd shrugged aside her objections. "Tell Cordell exactly what Mannie said. Your fiancé arrived in Cabo unexpectedly and you'd like to bring him to lunch. Put that way, he can hardly refuse."

Outgunned and outmaneuvered, Nina marched over to the counter and dialed the number Cordell had given her. To her profound dismay, he responded to her nervous request with urbane charm.

"But of course you must bring your friend. I look forward to meeting him."

He'd taken the bait, and now she was on the

hook! Hanging up the phone, she treated Blackstone to another glare.

"Okay. You're in."

"Good." He checked his watch. "We don't have much time. You'd better get cleaned up."

She managed not to slam the bedroom door behind her, but it took some effort. A hot shower and some judicious swipes of eye shadow and lip gloss erased most of the effects of her long night. Her hair presented a real challenge, however. She attacked it with a brush, tried a curling iron and finally decided to just twist up the heavy mass and anchor it with a clip.

What to wear presented another problem. The button-front linen sundress she'd worn yesterday— and most of the night, until she'd finally changed into shorts and a T-shirt—*looked* like she'd worn it all day and half the night.

She jammed the dress into a laundry bag with a slip requesting same-day service and reached for the multicolored, ankle-length cotton skirt she'd purchased her first day in Cabo. She teamed it with a red silk tank, added a rhinestone-studded belt that rode low on her hips, then slipped her feet into sandals.

"This is insane," she muttered to the image in the mirror. "Absolutely insane."

When she came out of the bedroom, Rafe was gripping a leather carryall. "One of Mannie's men retrieved my gear from my hotel. Won't take me long to clean up."

"We will leave now," the chief inspector said as Blackstone headed for the bedroom, "so we can be in position when you arrive."

"Position?" Nina echoed.

"El Lobo and I, we have had Cordell's hacienda under surveillance for several days. We listen, too, but Cordell is very cautious."

"You're not making me feel any better, Chief Inspector Diaz."

"You don't need to fear. We will be watching. And you will have El Lobo with you."

Somehow, that didn't exactly reassure her.

She was tapping a foot nervously when Wolf reappeared some fifteen minutes later. He'd showered and shaved and combed his damp black hair straight back.

Despite her jumpy nerves, Nina had to admit the man cleaned up *extremely* well. The wrinkled khakis had given way to pleated black slacks. The jungle print shirt was gone, thank goodness, replaced by a knit polo the same color as the sea at dusk. The deep color intensified the blue of his eyes. Not that they needed intensifying. Nina felt them on every inch of her body as he gave her a final once-over.

"Ready?"

"As I'll ever be."

"Did you call the desk and ask them to bring up your car?"

"Yes."

"Good girl. Let's get this show on the road."

Hot sun and blinding glare hit them the moment they walked out the door. Wincing, Nina slipped on her sunglasses. Rafe shielded his eyes with tinted aviator glasses. When they took the elevator up from the lower casita level and walked through the pyramid lobby, she saw Ramon was on duty again.

"Buenos dias, Dr. Grant."

"Buenos dias."

The parking valet gave her a cheerful smile before shifting his glance to Rafe. He was too well trained to comment on the fact that the man Nina had insisted would only be visiting her for a short time had stayed the entire night.

Nor did he question the order of things when Rafe walked around to the driver's side. With another friendly smile, the valet opened the passenger door for Nina. He already had the air conditioner blasting, so she sank into a welcome bath of chilled air.

"I hope you have a pleasant day."

"Thanks, Ramon. I hope so, too!"

As soon as Rafe had the rental pointed down the resort's long, winding drive, he fleshed out his role as the would-be love of her life.

"We have to assume Cordell has looked for you on Google. He'll know about your business and that you're on your way to becoming one of the wealthiest women under thirty in the United States. He may also have checked out this clown you planned to marry. Was there a public announcement of your engagement?"

"There was," she said with a wry twist to her lips. "My mother made sure it hit all the papers."

"Did the breakup hit the papers, too?"

"It did. We were at a restaurant when I confronted Kevin about the files he filched from my computer. He tried to bluster his way out of it, then got all huffy and patronizing, which made me even angrier."

She squirmed, embarrassed by the memory of the events that had followed.

"I dumped my wine in his lap. You would think that would send a strong enough signal, but he tried to stop me from walking out of the place. So I, uh, sort of slugged him."

Rafe shot her a quick glance. "Sort of?"

"I went for his chin," she confessed, her face flaming, "but he ducked and I popped him in the eye instead. Kevin stumbled back and tripped over a passing waiter with a full tray of drinks. They both went down." She let out a sigh. "Of course, the *Albuquerque Journal* society page editor had to be sitting in the next booth."

A smile played at the corner of Blackstone's mouth. "Of course."

"That was *not* my finest moment."

Laughter rumbled up deep and rich from her companion's chest. "Sounds damn fine to me. I'm just glad you missed *my* eyes with those keys last night."

He should laugh more, Nina thought. *Or maybe not.* That wicked grin did things to her insides she had no business feeling.

"Tell me about this guy Kevin," he said, still chuckling. "Where's he from? What does he do?"

"He's an investment advisor and financial planner."

"Likes to play with other people's money, does he?"

"He does. He also likes to tool around in vintage sports cars."

She spent most of the drive into town detailing her former fiancé's background and wondering all over again how she could have fallen for such a wimp.

Not that Kevin was a lightweight. At six one, he packed as much muscle on his frame as Wolf did. It was just distributed differently. A little less at the shoulders, a little more at the waist. They both had dark hair, too, although Kevin's had already started to thin on top.

Yet despite their outward similarities, the two men possessed distinctly different personalities. Blackstone telegraphed a quiet assurance and an inbred toughness that Kevin couldn't achieve if he popped B-12 and pumped iron for the rest of his life.

"I've got the picture," Wolf said as they approached the roundabout and the turnoff for the road to Cordell's distant hacienda. "You got engaged to a glorified accountant with a taste for flashy cars, which he tried to pay for by stealing proprietary data from your computer."

She bristled but quickly deflated. Hard to argue with the truth. "That about sums it up."

"He's lucky he got off with a punch in the eye,"

Wolf commented as he slowed for the circle. He had to maneuver carefully to avoid the souvenir hawkers who darted out to flash trays of silver bracelets and rings at the tourists cruising by. "You could have... Well, hell!"

"What's the matter?"

"We forgot a ring."

"I don't need a ring. We're unengaged, remember?"

"Previously unengaged, currently reunited."

"Not reunited enough for me to be wearing your ring. Besides, if what you told me is true, a wedding band didn't stop Cordell from going after Senator DeWitt."

"True. But her husband stayed home in Maine, while she played with her lover in Washington. Cordell won't find it as easy to get around me."

With that dubious reassurance, he exited the traffic circle and took the road leading to Cordell's distance hacienda.

This talk about engagement rings and wedding bands left Nina prey to some very confused emotions. Frowning, she stared down at her naked ring finger and tried to come to grips with her thoughts.

Kevin had picked out the diamond he'd slipped on her finger. Round cut and mounted on a fussy, filigreed band, it wasn't a ring she would have chosen herself. Still, after he'd gone down on one knee and presented it with a goofy grin, she'd drifted for weeks on a tide of happy dreams of their life together.

Now, here she was—no Kevin, no ring. Certainly no happy dreams to follow. And she didn't care.

She really didn't care.

Relief washed through Nina in waves as she realized she'd put Kevin out of her life *and* out of her heart. The tumultuous events of the past twenty four hours—and a certain obnoxious special agent—had crowded Kevin completely aside.

She slanted Rafe Blackstone a quick glance. She still owed him for scaring her last night. Nor was she happy about the way he'd strong-armed her into taking this jaunt into the countryside. El Lobo had certainly injected more excitement than she'd anticipated or wanted into her enforced vacation.

Then there was the matter of his startling transformation. Despite his bristles and gaudy tropical shirt, he'd looked hot as hell last might. Minus the bristles, he was smokin'. Far too sexy for any woman's peace of mind.

She shifted in her seat and sternly suppressed a ridiculous little twinge of regret that their pretend engagement would end the moment they departed Cordell's hacienda.

Assuming they got in, that is. She knew Rafe planned to plant some kind of listening device. Maybe more than one. He had the bugs with him. Somewhere. God knew what else he had on him.

Nina grew more anxious about that with each mile. Those armed guards with holsters tucked into their armpits had made a distinct impression on her yesterday. She tried not to obsess over the guns. Tried *very* hard.

In desperation, she focused on the passing countryside. It looked the same as it had when she'd driven through it the first time. Tall cactus, spiny creosote, a scattering of green-leafed trees hugging the few streams and creeks that cut through the otherwise parched hills.

Along one stretch of the road, the trees dripped with vines sprouting bright yellow flowers. She hadn't noticed the showy blossoms yesterday. Then again, she'd been more concerned with the coughing coming from her car engine than the local flora and fauna.

Despite her determined search for distraction, Nina had worked up a bad case of the jitters by the time Cordell's compound appeared on a distant hill. With its red tile roof and cream-colored adobe, the sprawling hacienda looked so inviting, so enticing, set on its cliff above the sea.

Their host was expecting them, she reminded herself nervously. Surely the guards would escort them right to the house. Or would they? Remembering how they'd searched her tote, she glanced uneasily toward Wolf.

"You're not armed, are you?"

He shrugged. "Not with anything Cordell's thugs will discover if they pat me down."

Chapter 5

Great. Wonderful. Marvelous.

Here she was—neat, precise, always-in-control Nina Grant—at this very moment pulling up to the gates of a compound with a man packing some sort of lethal weapon that couldn't be discovered by a pat-down.

Never, ever, in her wildest imagination would she have pictured herself in this situation. Her employees wouldn't believe when she told them about it. *If* she lived to tell them about it.

For several panicky moments Nina seriously considered informing Blackstone that she'd changed her mind. No government contract was worth either life or limb. His terse assertion last night that this was a matter of national security made her hesitate.

Then it was too late. The security cameras mounted at strategic angles above the gates blinked red and Rafe leaned out the window to hit the call button.

"*Sí?*"

He responded to the gruff query. "Dr. Nina Grant and Mr. Kevin James to see Mr. Cordell."

"Wait there. Someone comes."

The window whirred up again, enclosing them in a cool cocoon that did little to soothe Nina's increasingly frazzled nerves.

"I bet they're going to search my bag again. They'll check you, too."

Twisting in her seat, she skimmed a nervous glance over his knit shirt and pleated slacks. She couldn't spot any bulges. Except one, and that was right where it should be. Hastily, she raised her eyes.

"Are you sure they won't find anything?"

"I'm sure."

The reply was calm and reassuring. Until a very belated thought hit her.

"Oh, Lord! They asked me for some identification the first time. What if they ask to see *your* ID?"

"Not a problem. The people I work with took care of that while you were in the shower."

"How in the world…?" She shook her head. "Never mind! I don't want to know!"

"Relax, Nina." He flicked a casual glance at the cameras still aimed in their direction. "We're being watched, remember?"

"Like I could forget?"

He shifted in his seat and stretched an arm along the back of hers. Those blue eyes lanced into her. "You're wound tight, aren't you? You need a distraction."

"You think?"

"Let's try this."

With calm deliberation, he curled his arm around her shoulders. Nina had a moment, just a moment, to grasp his purpose as he angled her as far as her seat belt would allow and leaned across the console.

She could have pulled back. His hold was loose enough, his intention clear. Sheer surprise held her still—coupled with a overwhelming and completely irrational hunger to feel his mouth on hers.

She got her wish. The kiss started light, casual, a leisurely exploration of her mouth with his. She had no idea whether he deepened it or she did, but someone certainly upped the stakes. Next thing she knew, her palms were splayed against the muscled contours of his chest and the lips that had merely toyed with hers suddenly came down hard. Demanding instead of coaxing. Taking as much as they gave.

Swift and unexpected, a searing heat shot through her. It came in a short, intense burst that curled her toes against the soles of her sandals. Her rational mind said this was crazy, that Rafe Blackstone was a stranger, and a dangerous one at that. The rest of her thrilled to the taste and the feel and the scent of him.

He was the first to draw back. Fighting for breath, Nina was happy to see that the kiss had disconcerted him as much as it had her. The skin across his cheeks was stretched tight. A deep groove creased his forehead.

"Mission accomplished," she got out on a shaky breath. "Consider me officially distracted."

The crease carved deeper into his brow. "Christ, Nina, I'm…"

The rattle of the electronic gate swinging back on its hinges cut him off. Muttering a curse, he withdrew his arm and shifted to face front.

The driver of the Hummer that pulled up beside them was the same guard who'd driven Nina back to her rental car yesterday. He leaned out the window, his dark eyes raking over them. Despite Rafe's assurances—and very potent distraction—Nina gouged her nails into her palms while the guard in the passenger seat climbed out.

"You will step out of the car, please, so I may look inside."

The searing heat sucked away what little air Nina had left in her lungs, but her hands got cold and clammy as the guard checked the rental's interior and bent to look under the seats before popping the trunk. When he extracted a long pole with a mirror attached from the back of the Hummer and examined the rental's undercarriage, Wolf shook his head in a very credible show of disbelief and amusement.

"What's with all this? Does your boss think my fiancée and I are terrorists or something?"

"Señor Cordell is a very powerful man. He has many friends, and many who envy him his possessions. He takes no chances."

"Yeah, I see that."

"Dr. Grant, I must check your bag."

"Okay."

The guy pawed through her tote, then set it aside. Nina thought her heart would stop when he turned to Wolf and asked him to hold out his arms.

"You're kidding, right?"

"No, *señor.*"

With a shrug, Blackstone extended his arms. Nina didn't draw a single breath until the guard finished with him and gestured them back to their vehicle.

"Please follow us up to the hacienda."

She dropped into her seat. This was *not* her idea of a restful vacation.

"Are you going to tell me what kind of supersecret weapon you're carrying? It would be nice to know, if you whip it out and I need to duck or something."

"I'm not carrying anything. You might want to give me the little plastic bottle I slipped in your tote, though. Looks like ordinary hand sanitizer," he added helpfully.

Her jaw dropped. She had to struggle for words. "You...you used me? As a *mule?*"

"We didn't have a whole lot of time to improvise this morning. I figured you're more the hand sanitizer type than I am."

Flabbergasted, Nina could only gape at him. In a few short hours, Rafe Blackstone had turned her world upside down. Not to mention putting her on an emotional roller coaster. In rapid succession, she'd progressed from lusting for him to fearing him to loathing him to wishing the kiss a few seconds ago lasted a whole lot longer.

Now anger topped the list again. A nice, cleansing rage, that had her diving into her tote and winding up to fling the plastic bottle at his head.

"Careful! That stuff can be volatile."

Her hand jerked to a stop. Carefully, very carefully, she deposited the container on his outstretched palm.

"What *is* that?" she demanded as he slipped it into his shirt pocket.

"Nothing you need to worry about right now. We're almost there."

Wild thoughts of explosive gels and/or nerve-paralyzing agents rushed through her mind as El Lobo brought the rental to a stop inside the flower-filled courtyard.

Cordell had come out to greet them. Elegant in white slacks, a slim belt, and a pale blue silk shirt with his monogram on the pocket, he strolled forward to open Nina's door. She had to dig deep for a smile when he helped her out and raised her hand to his lips.

"I'm so pleased you could join me, Dr. Grant. And you, Mr. James," he added when Blackstone exited the rental.

"Thanks for including me in the invitation."

The two men engaged in that time-honored male ritual of crunching each other's digital phalanges while sizing up the competition.

"I gather from Nina's call this morning that your trip to Cabo was somewhat spur of the moment."

Nodding, her pretend fiancé looped an arm around her shoulders. She didn't have to feign unease or nervousness. Or the residual temper that made her shrug out of his loose embrace. She'd be a long time forgetting that plastic bottle of whatever he'd slipped into her tote.

If Sebastian Cordell noted the deliberate disengagement, he didn't comment on it. Instead, he ushered them through a vine-draped breezeway and into the wide, double-doored entrance to the main building.

Nina had only seen portions of the interior on her previous visit, but that was enough to prepare her for Cordell's masterful blend of contemporary and antique. Despite her nervousness, she drank in the beauty of his book-lined study, which showcased an Italian Rococo desk topped by a sleek computer with a twenty-inch monitor. In a sunken living room the size of a football field, an Italian rococo armoire housed a state-of-the art sound system. The white leather-and-chrome sectional sofa was positioned opposite a glass wall with a spectacular view of the sea.

But it was the man's art collection that once again stopped the breath in Nina's throat. She'd always been more into science than art, but even her untrained eyes recognized masterpieces when she saw them. Sculptures in bronze and marble held places of honor on pedestals and in subtly lit niches. Paintings—some small and exquisitely framed, some wall size—ran the gamut from soft, dreamy impressionist landscapes to bold, almost violent slashes of color.

"I told the staff to serve lunch on the terrace." Their host gestured toward a set of sliding glass doors that framed a vista of sparkling fountains, marble statues and colorful bougainvillea. "It's shaded and cooled by the sea breeze, but we can eat inside if you prefer."

"No," Nina breathed awed in spite of herself by the glorious setting, "the terrace looks perfect."

Wolf made a slight movement on her other side. She threw him a quick look and remembered belatedly that the whole reason for this visit was to give him a chance to scope out the inside of the hacienda.

Well, hell! Five minutes into her role as a

modern day Mata Hari and she'd already flubbed it. Kicking herself, Nina tried to recover.

"Unless… Uh… Kevin hasn't had time to acclimate to the Cabo sun. Maybe we should eat inside."

"Kevin" shook his head. "Outside is fine."

"Are you sure?" Cordell asked graciously. "The enclosed portion of the terrace has an equally fine view."

"I'm sure."

"Very well." He slid back one of the glass doors and took Nina's elbow. "Shall we have an aperitif first? Since moving to Mexico, I've invented a most refreshing drink that consists of equal parts lime juice and *Pasión Azteca*."

"*Pasión Azteca,*" she murmured, fighting not to flinch away from his touch. "That sounds very exotic."

"It is. Quite exotic, I assure you."

He ushered them along a passage shaded by vines woven through white latticework.

"Most aficionados believe *Pasión Azteca* is the world's finest tequila. It's made from the pure sap of the blue agave plant that's been fermented, distilled, and aged for more than six years. The bottles themselves are limited edition works of art, done in silver, gold or platinum."

"Platinum? You're kidding!"

"Not at all. Each bottle is individually designed and engraved by Alejandro Gomez Oropeza, one of Mexico's greatest artists."

The husky note in his voice told Nina he really got off on this stuff. That, and the slow up-and-down stroke he gave her arm.

"A platinum edition of *Pasión Azteca* sold at auction last month for well over two hundred thousand dollars. I foolishly let myself be outbid on that one but I have my people looking for another. Today, I'm sad to say, we must make do with a silver edition."

His "make do" bottle sat in splendor on a wheeled bar cart tended by a servant in a white jacket and gloves. Shaped like a spiked sea shell, the bottle gleamed in the few rays that managed to sneak past the vines shading the terrace.

"Three glasses with ice, Enrique. I shall mix the drinks myself."

"*Sí*, Señor."

With Wolf beside her, Nina watched a master at work. Thankfully, it looked as though he added more fresh squeezed lime juice than tequila to the crystal martini shaker. The last thing she needed was to get a buzz on and say or do something stupid.

She realized the error of her thinking as soon as she took the first sip from a long-stemmed glass. This baby tasted nothing like the drinks at the Purple Parrot. Or anywhere else, for that matter.

Marvelously smooth and deceptively gentle, the tequila-tini glided down her throat. She didn't feel its lethal bite until a few moments later, when they were seated at a vine-shaded table and had the Sea of Cortez in all its mesmerizing beauty laid out before them.

"I have a confession to make, Dr. Grant," Cordell said with a smile. "Or may I call you Nina?"

"Yes, of course."

"And you must call me Sebastian." He twirled his glass, his pale blue eyes drifting from her to Wolf and back again. "After you appeared at my gates yesterday and gave me your card, I looked for you on Google."

Oh, God! Here it comes.

Her stomach lurching, Nina was sure she and El Lobo were about to be exposed as complete frauds. She had visions of her companion whipping out his hand sanitizer and squirting their way out of the compound when Cordell gave her an approving smile.

"I'm quite impressed by your business acumen, my dear. Grant Medical Data Systems is perfectly positioned to ride what most experts predict will be the wave of the future in health care data sharing."

"I certainly hope so."

Cordell's beautifully manicured hand twirled the glass stem again. "From what I read, less than half your funding derives from private sources, with the majority coming from government contracts."

Heroically, Nina managed to refrain from shooting El Lobo an evil glare. "That's true."

"I may be able to help you increase your slice of the government pie. Although I now reside in Mexico, I still have a good many friends in Washington."

One of whom was now extremely dead.

Hastily, Nina masked the grim reminder of Senator DeWitt behind another sip of tequila.

"Perhaps you should provide me with a complete company prospectus and five-year plan," Cordell said smoothly. "I'll make sure it gets in the hands of people who can make things happen."

Sure he would. The man had to be drinking something a whole lot more potent than blue agave sap if he thought she was going to give him access to her company's finances. She was framing a polite refusal when Blackstone laid a possessive arm across the back of her chair.

"That's exactly what I've been telling Nina. She needs to exploit any and all business contacts. I sure would."

This time she couldn't restrain a glare. He was cutting his role as her scumbag ex-fiancé a little too close to the bone.

"Yes," their host agreed, "I imagine you would. You're in the investment and financial planning arena, aren't you?"

"Did you get that off Google, too?"

"I did." A smile flitted across Cordell's tanned face. "Along with a rather descriptive account of the termination of your engagement to Nina. How fortunate for you she took you back."

"She says she's still thinking about it," Wolf replied with a wink, "but I'm ninety-nine-point-nine-percent sure of the outcome."

When he gave her shoulder a squeeze, Cordell dipped his head in a benign nod. "I wish you luck."

It was all so civilized, so polite. Yet Nina couldn't shake the nasty feeling she was a small, brown mouse being batted between the paws of two very powerful and very predatory jungle cats.

"It was a long ride out here," Rafe said, interrupting her uneasy thoughts. "Guess you'd better point me in the direction of a bathroom."

"Of course. There's one in the pool cabana at the other end of the terrace. Or you may go back inside the house and to your left."

"Thanks. Mind if I take a look at some of your bronzes while I'm at it? I'm something of a collector myself."

"Are you? Then I must give you a guided tour after lunch."

"Great."

When Wolf headed for the sliding glass doors, Nina had to swallow a panicky urge to call him back. This was what he'd come for, why he'd coerced her into acting as his entree into Cordell's compound. Now that she knew about her smooth-talking host's dark past, however, she didn't particularly relish being left alone with him. She did her best to hide her unease as he leaned back in his chair and regarded her with slow consideration.

"I hope I didn't embarrass you by bringing up that article about the termination of your engagement."

"I'm well past being embarrassed by it."

"Yet I sense... Forgive me if I'm getting too personal." His gaze dropped to her ringless left hand and lingered a moment before lifting to her face. "I sense you and Kevin haven't quite repaired the, shall we say, cracks in the road that led to your breakup."

"We're working on them."

"I see." He drummed his fingers on the tabletop, the picture of friendly concern. "Would you like a word of advice from one who's tasted great passion a few times in his life?"

At her cautious nod, he stretched out an arm and laid his hand over hers.

"Someone as young and beautiful as you shouldn't have to work at love."

Right, she thought scornfully, *for "young", read "gullible". For "beautiful", try "well off".* In a patently obvious attempt to change the subject, she eased her hand from under his and gestured to a gleaming yacht anchored a few hundred feet from the rock cliffs.

"Is that your boat?"

"It is. Would you like to take a cruise aboard her?"

"Well... I..."

"And Kevin, of course. Assuming he's going to remain here in Cabo with you."

"I don't know. We, uh, need to work on those cracks you mentioned."

"I have commitments tomorrow, but I could take you out Thursday morning. I've already instructed my crew to have the boat ready for a sea voyage later in the day. How does that work for you?"

"Let me think about it."

Desperate, she resorted to polite chitchat about the weather and the crowds in Cabo until Wolf reappeared. She greeted his return with relief. Let him get us out of this entanglement!

"Sebastian has offered to take us out for a spin in his boat."

His glance shot to the yacht anchored offshore. "By boat, I hope you mean that beauty."

"She does, indeed," Sebastian answered. "As I told Nina, however, I couldn't do it until Thursday afternoon." His hooded gaze locked with Wolf's. "Will you be staying in Cabo until then?"

Even Nina, as jittery as she was, sensed Cordell had thrown down a gauntlet. His opponent picked it up without missing a beat.

"Damn straight I will."

Oh, Lord! He wanted to take Cordell up on his offer! She could see it in his eyes, read it in the speculative glance he gave the gleaming white yacht.

There was absolutely no way she was heading out to sea on that monster, pretty as it was. She got seasick in the bathtub, for pity's sake. She leaned back, out of Cordell's line of sight, and telegraphed a silent but unmistakable *no!*

Her "fiancé" acknowledged the frantic signal with a small nod and proceed to completely ignore it.

"Thursday works great for us, doesn't it, Pumpkin? We didn't have anything heavier on the agenda than soaking up some rays at the pool. What time do you want us here, Sebastian?"

Chapter 6

Riding a wave of fierce elation, Wolf took a last look at the cliffside compound in the rearview mirror.

He'd managed to plant two listening devices—one in Cordell's study and one behind a painting of what looked like rotting fruit. In the process, he'd burned the layout and dimensions of each room he'd passed through into his brain. He'd also scouted the grounds. If he had to go back into the compound, he knew exactly how he would do it.

That was looking more and more necessary. All indications were Cordell intended to move the technology he'd stolen from Senator DeWitt's office within the next few days. Interpol, the CIA, and military listening posts all over the world had picked up increasing chatter about interested buyers. Everyone from hostile heads of state to drug czars would kill to get their hands on the design for a new generation of ultrasmall, ultrasophisticated Unmanned Aerial Vehicles.

Compared to the UAV's currently flying combat missions in Iraq and Afghanistan, the new generation of drones would cost next to nothing. They would also be almost invisible in flight. If they performed even half as well as advertised, the fifteen-inch-long vehicles could weave through a jungle of skyscrapers, zoom under bridges and land on the balcony of a twenty-story apartment building.

They would also be so simple to operate, any pimply preteen could fly one loaded with, say, fifty kilos of cocaine from a jungle processing center in Colombia to the backyard of a dealer anywhere in the world. Wolf didn't even want to *think* about the lethal virus some nutcase could send through a window of the Oval Office.

"Pumpkin?"

Nina's sarcastic drawl cut through his swirling thoughts.

"Do I really strike you as the 'Pumpkin' type?"

Wolf shot her an incredulous look. Of all the lies and half-truths they'd just spun for Cordell, that was the one playing heaviest on her mind?

"It was kind of the spur of the moment," he admitted. "But now that you mention it…"

He made a quick visual sweep, from the strands of soft brown hair that had slipped free of her clip to the chili-pepper-red silk top shaping her breasts. After letting his gaze linger there a second or two longer than it should, Wolf brought his eyes back to hers.

"'Pumpkin' suits you. You're all soft and smooth, like a slice of Thanksgiving pie, but you pack enough spice to face Cordell down in his own lair."

"Thanks. I think."

She thinned her lips and gave him a taste of the spice he'd just mentioned.

"Incidentally, I don't appreciate the way you ignored my very obvious lack of desire to sail off into the sunset with Cordell."

"Sorry. I thought it best to keep all options open."

"I hope you don't think I intend to continue our charade until Thursday!"

"With any luck, this will be over before then."

By tonight, Wolf thought, if the devices he'd planted picked up any clues to where, when and how Cordell intended to dispose of his pilfered technology. Wire-tight with anticipation, he forced a smile.

"You did good today, Grant. Very good."

Oooh, boy, Nina thought. *There it was again.* The crooked grin that crinkled the skin at the corners of his eyes and almost made her forget Rafe had blackmailed her into acting as his entree into a viper's den. Steeling herself to resist its pull, she demanded clarification.

"So we're square? No more heavy-handed pressure about my government contracts?"

"We're square."

His reply should have satisfied her. She was off the hook. Done. Finito. She could go back to being merely a stressed-out exec on vacation.

So what the heck was with this sudden flat feeling? She wasn't Lara Croft, Tomb Raider, for Pete's sake! She'd just about wet herself when Cordell laid his hand over hers. All through lunch her stomach had been so knotted with tension she'd eaten maybe two bites of the *coquille St. Jacques* his chef had dished up. The entire time, she couldn't *wait* to get out of the hacienda. Out of this whole, weird scene Rafe Blackstone had dragged her into, kicking and screaming.

This sudden letdown was a natural reaction, she decided. Her system was readjusting itself, as did every stressed biological organism. Plants faced with drought conditions increased a key hormone called abscisic acid. Animals in tight situations reacted with abrupt changes in neurohormone levels. Their catecholamines and corticosteroids shot off the charts. Serotonin was suppressed.

She was just coming down after the pressure high of the past few hours, she told herself firmly. All she had to do was sit back and breathe. In. Out. In.

Unfortunately, every deep breath ratcheted up her awareness of the man beside her. Each whiff of the sun-warmed scent of his skin or the faint tang of his aftershave threw her neurohormones out of whack again.

She had them more or less under control by the time they approached the roundabout with the spin-off road leading to her resort. Then she noticed El Lobo spearing intent glances at the rearview mirror.

"What's the matter?"

"We've picked up a tail."

A tail! Good grief. Had she dropped into some alternate universe?

"He's been following us since we hit the outskirts of town," Wolf said calmly.

Her nervous system going berserk once more, Nina twisted around. The traffic in the circle was as chaotic as usual, with cars weaving in and out and trucks belching diesel fumes as they shifted gears.

"Which one is it?"

"Gray Chevy Aveo, three cars back, right lane."

While she searched the stream of traffic, her companion reached into his shirt pocket and flipped open his cell phone.

"Mannie, this is Wolf. I've got a Chevy Aveo on my ass. Is it one of your men?"

The response didn't appear to please him. He listened for another moment, keeping one hand on the wheel and one eye on the mirror.

"*Gracias, amigo.* I'll get back to you."

"Who is it?" Nina asked anxiously.

"Hang on a sec."

Holding his phone at eye level, he punched one button. A second later, he had the phone to his ear.

"Ace, this is Wolf. I need you to run a check on license number…"

He squinted into the mirror and reeled off the digits. Nina dug her nails into her palms until he flipped the phone shut again.

"What's going on? Who's Ace?"

"My controller. Same guy who arranged my new identity as your fiancé. Speaking of which…" He shot her a rueful grin. "We have a slight change in plans."

"*How* slight?"

"Mannie got a report of a repair order being called in for the flat screen TV in your suite at the Mayan Princess. A technician worked on it while we were at lunch."

"There wasn't…"

Her voice trailed off, then came back much weaker.

"There wasn't anything wrong with the TV last time I checked."

"Exactly."

He sounded so blasé! As if the possibility that a person or persons unknown had planted a bug in her hotel room was no more than a minor inconvenience.

Swallowing, she tried to grasp the implications. "Do you think Sebastian is behind this?"

"Probably. You're just his type. Smart. Beautiful. A power player."

She blinked, shaken out of her renewed bout of nerves. Smart and beautiful was better than soft and smooth. *Much* better. She basked in the compliment until Wolf added a casual kicker.

"I'm guessing Cordell wants to get a better picture of how things stand between you and me before he moves in for the kill."

"When you say kill, you *are* speaking metaphorically, aren't you?"

"Of course."

She might have believed him if not for a certain dead senator.

"Until we find out for sure what's going down," he continued with a sideways glance, "I'm afraid you're stuck with me. Think you can handle a few more hours?"

"I'll give it my best shot."

Her dry response in no way mirrored the quick flutter just under her ribs. Her thoughts zinged back to El Lobo's "distraction" just outside the gates of Cordell's compound. Then ahead, to the possibility he might have to distract her again. Her neurohormones skittering all over the place, Nina contemplated that possibility for the rest of the drive to the Mayan Princess.

* * *

Late afternoon had brought the resort to life. New arrivals waited in the open-air lobby to check in. Laughter and noisy splashes echoed from the crowded family pool on the lower level. Smiling waiters served tall, frosted drinks to couples lazing on double-wide lounges at the adult-only infinity pool on the upper level.

Just yesterday she'd been stretched out on one of those loungers and so bored she'd decided to drive out to see the countryside. In the twenty-four hours since, she'd stumbled into something right out of a James Bond movie. She couldn't quite believe she was now returning to her casita with an undercover operative to check it for bugs.

Unreal. Absolutely unreal.

"Act naturally," Wolf warned as they approached her unit. "If this TV repairman worked on anything besides the flat screen, we'll know soon enough."

"How?"

"Remember the woman I told you about? Our communications chief? Mackenzie Blair can pack more technology into a cell phone than NASA did into the Hubble telescope."

He proved his point once they were inside. While Nina made straight for the fridge and a bottle of chilled water, he flipped up his phone.

"I need to check my voice mail," he said casually.

He kept his jazzed-up Hubble telescope at his ear and appeared to be listening intently while he paced the living area before strolling out onto the balcony. Nervous as a cat, Nina watched him lean a hip against the railing that framed the triangular hot tub. A sudden and very explicit vision grabbed her by the throat.

El Lobo. Her. In the hot tub. Naked. With a full moon reflected in a dark, shimmering sea.

She chugged down her water, half scared, half hoping he would find a bug that would force him to play her would-be lover just a *little* bit longer.

He did. Two, in fact. One in the living room, one in the bedroom. Both very sophisticated and high tech, but no match for the gizmo Wolf aimed at them.

Signaling Nina to join him in the bedroom, he gave her a status report. "I left the one in the living room active," he said in a low voice, "but scrambled the signal on this one. Whoever is listening will think it malfunctioned."

"Who *is* listening?"

"I should have the answer to that shortly. I've requested a signal intercept. Until we get a fix on it…"

Her heart skipped a beat.

"…we need to continue our respective roles."

She gathered the folds of her colorful broom skirt in her fists, bombarded once again by the image of the two of them in the hot tub. Naked. Etc.

"Relax," he said with a smile that produced the exact opposite of its intended effect. "I don't expect you to perform for the cameras."

"That's a relief."

Damn! Why couldn't she lie with a straight face like everyone else? She could feel the heat coloring her cheeks as Blackstone outlined his plan of attack.

"Here's the deal. We amble back into the living room. I comment on the long drive back from Cordell's and suggest a drink up at the pool. You counter with that old stand-by 'we need to talk'. I agree, but insist we can do that poolside as easily as we can here. We change, slather on some sunscreen, and move out of listening range."

The plan was simple enough. Nina even managed to inject a note of authenticity into her assigned line of dialogue. If Wolf were Kevin, they certainly would have to talk.

The first glitch occurred when he walked out of the bedroom wearing a pair of low-riding gym shorts and not much else. The second, when he took the bottle of sun lotion from her suddenly nerveless hand.

"I'll do your back."

He did her back *and* neck *and* arms *and* thighs. Nina wasn't sure her knees would keep her upright when it was her turn to perform the same service.

"Turn around."

He obliged and presented a broad back that tapered to a lean waist and a very tight, very trim butt. Eyeing it appreciatively, she oozed lotion into her palm. The sunscreen was cool and creamy, in direct contrast to her throat, which got hotter and drier with every swipe of her hands over his back and shoulders.

She tried to remind herself this was all for show, that Blackstone's only intention was to keep up the pretense. The stern reminder didn't prevent her fingers from gliding over his back longer than was absolutely necessary to work in the sunscreen.

"There." Swallowing to lubricate her bone-dry throat, she capped the bottle. "That should do you."

"Thanks."

He didn't turn around, just stared at the doors to

the balcony. "Why don't you go on up to the pool? I'll follow in a minute."

Oh, God! Now what? Imagining all kinds of disasters, she grabbed her tote and cover-up and fled the scene.

Wolf heard the door shut behind her but didn't move. He couldn't. The woman's slow, sensual strokes had damn near paralyzed him. Half of him, anyway.

Above the waist his lungs were so tight and frozen he had to fight to suck in air. Below the waist...

He was tight there, too, but certainly not frozen. Hunger burned hot and fierce in his belly. Swearing, he gritted his teeth and glared at the endless expanse of ocean beyond the balcony.

As if he didn't have enough to contend with. One dead United States senator. Stolen technology up for grabs to the highest bidder. A disaster in the making for U.S. national security. Now he had to go and develop a serious case of lust for Dr. Nina Grant.

She wasn't even his type, for God's sake! Too nice. Too damn gullible. Wolf had always gone for the kind of woman who didn't expect—or particularly want—him to hang around. The kind he could kiss goodbye and forget, once he'd completed an op. Nina, he suspected, wasn't the forgetting kind.

More to the point, she represented everything he'd deliberately avoided during his years with OMEGA. Ties. Commitments. Responsibilities that might shade his judgment when he went into dangerous situations. Although Wolf had seen many of his fellow agents successfully combine undercover work and marriage, the effort took its toll. Most left the business eventually. He just hadn't met the woman he wanted to make the switch for.

This one, though, stirred all kinds of thoughts he had no business thinking. Setting his jaw, Wolf willed his body into submission. He had to remember where he was. Had to stay focused on the mission. There was too much at stake to indulge in his ferocious urge to drag Ms. Grant back down to her suite, peel off her bathing suit, and bury himself between her lotion-slick thighs.

With another smothered curse, Wolf stalked out of the casita. His phone buzzed just as the door slammed behind him. He glanced at the coded ID on the display, flipped up the lid, and snarled into the mouthpiece.

"What?"

"Wolf?" Ace asked sharply. "You okay?"

"Yeah." Gritting his teeth, he moderated his tone. "What have you got?"

"The tag on the Chevy Aveo checks to Economy Rentals at the Cabo airport. They leased it this morning to one Anton Hdrovski. The name's fake. Ditto the passport he registered with them."

"Did you get a visual from airport surveillance?"

"We did. No positive ID yet, but this character sure looks like Ivan Alekseev. Heavier build. Less hair. Same ugly sneer."

Wolf's gut took another twist. A suspected lieutenant in the Russian mafia, Alekseev reportedly ran a host of illegal activities. Everything from drugs and black market military weaponry to white slavery.

So far, Interpol hadn't been able to nail him. Wolf had never worked in his area of operations, but he knew at least two Interpol agents had died trying to infiltrate the Russian's tight inner circle. The fact that Alekseev had appeared on the scene upped the stakes considerably.

"How did Alekseev pick up my tail?" he asked, grimly.

"Actually, we think he was tailing Dr. Grant. Once we ID'ed him, Mannie Diaz shook down some of his sources. They confirm the Russian heard from *his* sources here in Cabo that Cordell invited an American woman to his compound for lunch. Alekseev was too late to follow her to the hacienda, but he caught her on the way back into town."

"Hell!" Wolf considered a dozen possibilities, none of them good. "Sounds like Alekseev thinks she might be another potential buyer, or acting for one."

"Sounds like."

His jaw locked. He didn't need Ace to spell it out for him. If Alekseev and company believed Nina was a player in Cordell's auction, they could well decide to eliminate the competition.

"What about the signals emanating from the bug in Dr. Grant's suite? Did you run the intercept?"

"We did. They're low frequency, with a limited range."

Which meant whoever was listening could be close enough to have his ear to the wall. His spine crawling, Wolf made a slow three sixty.

"Mac's still working the intercept," Ace told him. "She said to give her a few more hours. She's confident she'll be able to lock in on the listening post."

He hoped to hell she did. The ultraluxurious

casitas were stacked one on top of the other, clinging to the cliff face below the towering pyramid of the main building. There must be close to a hundred of them. One-, two- and three-bedroom units, in shades of umber and ochre that blended in with the cliffs themselves.

He could help at this end, he decided. He'd get with hotel management. Find out who checked into which units in the past twenty-four hours. In the meantime…

"Lightning wants you to stick close to Dr. Grant," Ace reported. "Intentionally or not, she's becoming a key player in this op."

And he'd forced her into it.

Wolf had never hesitated to employ whatever tools necessary to accomplish a mission, but this particular tool was starting to play on his conscience, big time. He didn't need Lightning's instructions. He intended to stick *extremely* close to Nina Grant. Day and night.

Chapter 7

Infiltrating Sebastian Cordell's compound with a fake fiancé in tow had pretty well maxed out Nina's fun meter. That exercise was a stroll on the beach, however, compared to having her fake fiancé stretched out next to her on a double-wide lounger.

An absorbent, cloth-covered mattress at least four inches thick cushioned the lounger. A roll made of the same cushiony material served as a pillow. With her head propped on the roll, Nina had an unobstructed view across a seamless blend of turquoise pool and achingly blue ocean.

Unobstructed, that is, except for a bent knee.

Which connected to a hard, muscled thigh. Which connected to the hip that bumped hers as Wolf settled in beside her.

"I just talked to my people. They—and I—think it's best if we remain engaged until Cordell makes his move. Or at least for the duration of your stay in Cabo. When are you supposed to head home?"

"My assistant booked me for an entire week."

Very much against her will.

Talk about irony. When her staff had threatened to resign en mass if she didn't take some time off, Nina had reminded them of all the hot projects they had in the works and insisted she couldn't drop everything and jet off to Mexico. Even after she'd caved and arrived here at the Mayan Princess, she hadn't been able to relax. Too many things on her mind, too much restless energy.

Rafe Blackstone had certainly tapped into that energy. And something deeper. More urgent. She wanted to believe it was a sense of outrage over Cordell's alleged role in Senator DeWitt's death, but she knew darn well the naked chest just inches from her nose factored heavily into the equation.

"I don't fly home until Saturday," she told him. "I, uh, could stay longer if you need me."

The cushion dipped as he propped himself up on an elbow and tipped his mirrored sunglasses.

Surprise and a touch of amusement played in his blue eyes.

"Is this the same Nina Grant who made me swear not more than a half hour ago that we're all square?"

"It is," she said loftily. "Just because I dislike being blackmailed doesn't mean I won't do whatever I can to help expose a traitor."

"I appreciate the offer, but as I told you in the car, this should be over soon."

"What if it's not?" It was Nina's turn to tip her sunglasses. "Don't you think it's about time to tell me what, exactly, Sebastian intends to auction off to the highest bidder?"

Wolf had to make a split-second decision. Grant wasn't cleared for the level of detail she now demanded. He could stonewall her—or bring her fully into the op. He went with his instinct.

First, though, he speared a quick glance around the pool. They weren't the only couple soaking up the late afternoon rays but none of the others were anywhere close enough to overhear. Nevertheless, Wolf kept his voice low as he described the new generation Unmanned Aerial Vehicles at risk because Janice DeWitt hiked up her skirt, shimmied out of her thong panties, and had sex with the man she knew as Stephen Caulder atop her desk in the Russell Senate Office Building.

With her PhD in biology, Nina grasped the devastating potential of the stolen technology immediately. Her eyes went wide with dismay.

"If these UAVs are as inexpensive to build and easy to fly as you say, some wild-eyed terrorist could deliver a deadly strain of anthrax or ebola anywhere on the planet."

"Just about."

"No wonder you resorted to kidnapping and blackmail to gain entree into Cordell's compound!"

She swiped her tongue across her lips, clearly trying to take it all in. Wolf half expected her to reneg on her offer at that point. As he'd related to Ace after the frustrating prep session, Dr. Nina Grant didn't have the temperament for undercover work. So her angled chin and terse reply took him by surprise.

"Count me in, Blackstone. I'll do whatever I can to help put Cordell behind bars where he belongs."

"You sure?" Now that he'd secured her willing cooperation, Wolf was hit with a fierce need to talk her out. "We're playing for extremely high stakes, Nina. People could get hurt."

She paled, but nodded. "I'm sure."

Her declaration shifted something inside Wolf. He couldn't quite identify the odd sensation. Probably because he'd never felt this combination of respect, admiration, guilt and fierce protectiveness before. All he knew at that moment was that he had to make her understand what she was up against.

Digging his elbow into the mattress, he leaned closer. She tilted into the crease and almost slid under him. His pelvis pressed into hers. His chest flatted her right breast. To any interested observer, they would project the image of a couple caught up in a very intimate conversation.

"You and I and Cordell aren't the only players in this game. My controller contacted me right before I came up to the pool. That tail we picked up...?"

Some of the bravado seeped out of her, replaced by a wary caution. "What about it?"

"From all indications, it was a real badass by the name of Ivan Alekseev. He's a major player in the Russian mafia."

Wolf saw her eyes widen behind her tinted lenses. She swallowed and said very carefully, "The Russians are following you?"

"Not me. You."

Her jaw dropped. *Me?*

"You." With brutal honesty, he laid the cards on

the table. "Mannie says Alekseev arrived in town just in time to hear from his sources that Cordell had invited a special guest to lunch. He's going to want to know who you are and what interest Cordell has in you."

The incredible news that she'd now become the focus of the Russian mafia shook Nina almost as much as lying chest to chest with Rafe.

"Wh…?" She struggled to sound coherent. "What do we do now?"

"Until I say otherwise, we do just what Nina and Kevin would do. We lie in the sun, we cool off in the pool, we have dinner, we take a moonlight strolls along the beach. In the process, we work out the kinks in our relationship."

Nina went into the pool several times in the hours that followed, but the cool turquoise water did little to soothe her frazzled nerves.

Particularly when Wolf rested his elbows beside hers on the pool's curved ledge. They floated side-by-side, massaged by the thin stream of water cascading over the lip. With nothing but that lip between them and the endless blue of the Pacific, they could have been alone in the universe.

Except, of course, for whoever might be watching. Or listening. Or trying to figure out if she was a player in Sebastian Cordell's dangerous game. The notion was absurd, and scary as hell. So scary that goose bumps popped out on her arms when she and Wolf abandoned the pool and went down to her casita to change for dinner.

The air-conditioned chill inside the casita piled another layer of goose bumps on top of the first. Shivering, Nina deposited her tote and wide-brimmed hat on the counter.

"I need to shower off the chlorine before dinner," she told him.

"Me, too."

"You want first crack at the bathroom?"

"No reason to take turns. I'll scrub your back, you scrub mine."

He delivered the suggestion in a caressing tone that squeezed the air from Nina's lungs. It took her several heart-stopping seconds to remember the bug behind the flat screen TV. Scrambling for a reason to decline the seductive offer, she shook her head.

"As tempting as that sounds, we'd better forego the back-scrubbing. We'll have to rush to make our dinner reservations as it is."

Was that a glint of approval for her quick thinking in his eyes? She couldn't quite decide, as he curled a knuckle under her chin.

"You wouldn't turn down a back scrub if you were really ready to forgive me."

"I'm still working on that," she said, fighting to remember her role as his thumb glided along her lower lip.

"Work harder. I'll do anything to get back into your heart, Pumpkin."

Oh, gag!

She didn't have any trouble interpreting the gleam in his eyes now. He was laughing at her.

Indignant, she fired back with a quick retort. "My heart, Kevin, or my bed?"

His thumb stilled. She had the satisfaction of seeing his amusement fade before she issued a tart warning.

"Don't push me, fella. I haven't had time to adjust to your unexpected appearance here in Cabo, much less your insistence we put the past behind us and start over. Let's just take this a day at a time."

"Guess we'll have to," he said after a moment. "You're calling the shots on this one."

His thumb glided over her lip one last time before he issued a warning of his own.

"Just don't expect me to roll over and play dead while you try to make up your mind about us. I want you, Nina. I didn't know how much until I lost you. I intend to do everything in my power to make you want me again, too."

Whoa! Playacting was one thing. Making her legs start to buckle and her heart thunder like the opening stanzas of Beethoven's Fifth was another. Scarcely able to breathe, Nina beat a hasty retreat to the bedroom.

Wolf let her go. Their hours at the pool had damn near shredded his concentration. Touching her, breathing in her chlorine-scented hair and skin had just about sent him over the edge.

Suppressing a savage oath, he hit the Play button on Nina's iPod and spun it to full volume before stalking out on the balcony. Another vicious spin brought the hot tub jets to noisy, bubbling life. His jaw locked, he contacted his controller.

"Ace, this is Wolf. Speak to me."

A cool shower and a change into the sleeveless sundress she'd had laundered and pressed helped Nina regain a semblance of her composure.

It slipped again when Wolf suggested they cancel their reservations at the resort's elegant dining room and eat at the open-air restaurant clinging to the cliff, just a hundred feet above the crashing waves.

"Good atmosphere," he murmured in her

ear, when he waved the hostess away to seat her himself, "and great cover. Still, it might be best to wait until we take that walk along the beach to shed our respective roles."

Good God! Did they have unseen observers watching them even here? Aiming some superbionic electronic ear their way from the top of the cliff or the balcony of one of the casitas?

Feeling hunted, Nina almost jumped out of her skin when Wolf bent lower and dropped a kiss just under her ear. Pure reflex had her hunching a shoulder and jerking quickly to one side.

"What are you doing?"

"Initiating the next phase of my campaign to make you forget the past and concentrate on our future."

Wolf reeled off the answer easily enough. Shaking off the lingering effect of that brief taste took considerably more effort.

It didn't help that Mackenzie had completed the signal intercept. According to Ace, the transmissions from the device behind the flat screen TV in Nina's living room traced to a receiver aboard one of the boats anchored in the Mayan Princess's protected cove.

Wolf could see it from where he sat. The twenty-foot runabout bobbed on the slowly darkening sea.

Who manned her? Who was listening? Cordell's henchmen? Alekseev's contacts? Or an unidentified third party? The uncertainty scraped at Wolf's nerves.

He'd find the answer. Later.

Right now he was still processing Ace's second bit of news. Turns out Cordell had taken a very interesting phone call in his study late this afternoon. The listening device Wolf had planted picked up every word. Slick as ever, Cordell couched his conversation to sound as though he was auctioning off one of his sculptures and indicated he was waiting to hear from one last buyer. The buyer had until noon tomorrow to put in his offer, then Cordell would close the deal and advise the successful bidder where and how to take delivery of the merchandise.

The clock was winding down, and with every second that ticked off Wolf's tension mounted. He was sick of waiting, tired of watching.

Putting a hard clamp on his impatience, he slipped back into the role of Nina's fiancé and scooted his chair over a few inches. His arm stretched across the back of hers. He kept his gaze on the spectacular sunset until a waiter materialized at their table.

"Would you like a drink before dinner?"

"We would." He gave Nina's shoulders an affectionate squeeze. "Let's have Champagne, Pumpkin, to celebrate our new beginning."

She didn't roll her eyes, but she came close. Despite the simmering tension, Wolf had to hide a grin as he placed the order.

"Cristal brut, 2002."

"Excellent choice, *señor.*"

"And very expensive," Nina commented as the waiter left to put in the order.

"You're worth it."

Nina would always blame the Champagne for what happened next. She didn't drink that much. A glass and a half. Two at most.

But those glasses hit hard. Probably because she'd taken only a few bites of breakfast and been too nervous to do more than sample the *coquilles St. Jacques* Cordell's chef had prepared for lunch. She tried to blunt the bubbly's impact with a Caesar salad mixed table side and succulent tilapia with angel hair pasta, but the heady sensation stayed with her right through a caramel crème brûlée to die for.

Wolf, damn him, exacerbated her tingly feeling at regular intervals with oh-so-casual touches. She knew he was merely performing his self-assigned role. That didn't stop the nerves just under her skin from dancing every time he touched her. Or keep her from quivering with anticipation at the idea of a moonlight stroll on the shore. Alone. Away from prying eyes or hidden devices.

Her anticipation mounted when they left the restaurant and approached the elevators. One bank ferried guests up to the resort's main lobby. Another whizzed them down the beach beyond the cliffs.

Wolf paused and gave her a choice. "You've had a helluva day. Are you too tired to take a walk?"

Nina prided herself on her common sense. She always thought things through, studied every option, made decisions only after considering all the facts. Every way she looked at the idea of a stroll along the beach with Wolf suggested she would be wise to take the out he offered. Wise, but dull, dull, dull. Tucking rational, deliberate Nina away for another day, she shrugged.

"After that sinful crème brûlée, I need a walk."

Ha! Who was she kidding? What she wanted was to lock her arms around Wolf's neck and drag him down into the surf, to make wild, passionate love à la Burt Lancaster and Deborah Kerr in *From Here To Eternity*.

All too vivid images of his naked body sprawled

atop hers haunted Nina as she and Wolf left a trail of footprints in the damp sand. Not until they reached a small cove some distance from the hotel and she'd kicked off her shoes to wade into the shallows did the images evaporate. The shock of a cold wave slapping her calves banished them instantly. No way she was dragging *anyone* into this chilly water to have her evil way with him!

With the surf foaming around her ankles, she headed for the shelter of the cove, but the now retreating wave cut the sand out from under her feet. She windmilled wildly and would have gone down if not for Wolf's quick reaction.

"Careful." He swept her up, out of the sucking sand and water. "The undertow can be treacherous along this stretch of coast."

Not just the undertow, she realized when he hefted her higher against his chest. The combination of moonlight, the relentless song of the sea and the feel of his arms around her was every bit as dangerous.

The skirt of her linen dress trailed in the surf as he carried her out of the water. She expected him to put her down once they'd gained higher ground. Instead, he stopped at the water's edge and stood there with her in his arms.

Surprised, Nina glanced up. The moon's glow

cast his features into sharp planes and angles. His jaw had locked, she saw, and the look in his eyes sent her already heightened senses into a joyous leap.

He wanted to kiss her, she saw with fierce elation, and not merely as a distraction this time! The desire was there, sudden and raw, more than matching her own.

As he had this morning outside Cordell's hacienda, Wolf gave her time to cry foul. One word, and he would have put her down. One slight tilt of her head away from his, and he would have ended it.

Nina had no intention of letting him end anything. She made that clear when she slid her free arm up to join the one she'd looped around his neck. He reacted to the glide of her palm over his chest and shoulder with a gruff warning.

"We're playing with fire here."

"I know."

When she tightened her arm, brought her mouth within an inch of his, he issued one last warning.

"This wouldn't be for show, Nina."

"God, I hope not!"

Chapter 8

With all due respect to Burt Lancaster and Deborah Kerr, making love on a moon- and sea-swept beach lacked certain basic amenities.

Like the assurance of privacy, for one thing. Although Nina estimated they'd walked a half mile or more from the Mayan's floodlit grounds, another couple might decide to take the same moonlight stroll. Or worse, the Russians Wolf said were scoping her out.

Then there was the small matter of sand fleas. Nina didn't notice them nipping at her bare toes right away. She was too aroused, too eager to touch and be touched.

Wolf didn't appear to notice them, either. Burying a hand in her hair, he anchored her head for his kiss. His other hand slid down her back to cup her bottom and urge her closer. They stood chest to chest, pelvis to pelvis, straining against each other while his hand roamed her derriere.

"I was right," he murmured against her lips. "You're as soft and smooth as—"

She interrupted him with an indignant huff. "You'd better not be going where I think you're going with that!"

Laughing, he avoided any further reference to pumpkins and dipped his head to kiss the slopes of her breasts above the neckline of her sundress. When he eased open the top few buttons for greater access, Nina sucked in a swift breath. Her stomach hollowed at the rasp of his tongue on her bare skin. The sensation was so erotic she had to dig her fingers into his shoulders to steady herself.

Her shaky legs gave out a few moments later, right along with her ability to withstand his assault on her senses. She sank to her knees in the soft sand. He followed, holding her close. She could feel him rock hard and jutting against her stomach. The sensual pressure tightened her own belly and sent spirals of dark, hot pleasure spinning through her.

She was panting when he tumbled her down to

the sand. Her dress flared out like a beach blanket and should have protected her more from most uninvited guests. Four wiggles and a hard slap later, she recognize the error of her thinking.

"I'm being eaten alive."

"That's the plan," Wolf said with a look that curled her toes into the sand. "But maybe we should adjourn to the resort first."

They made the twenty-minute walk back to the Mayan Princess in ten. As swift as the hike was, it gave Wolf the time he need to recirculate the blood that had emptied out ofhis brain and pooled below his waist.

He had to be out of his mind. He'd had a taste of what this woman could do to him earlier this afternoon. He knew better than to play with fire like this. Letting down his guard for even a few minutes was a good way to get real dead, real fast.

He was in the midst of an op, for God's sake. He had a boat anchored less than a hundred yards off shore. Men hunched over a receiver, tuned in to any sounds emanating from Nina's casita. Yet all Wolf could think of was hauling her back to the suite and getting her naked.

Nina Grant had him tied in knots like none he'd

ever learned in the navy. He'd damn well better take control of the situation. Rein in his raging hunger and in the process bring her down carefully, gently.

He had every intention of doing exactly that. Even when they reached the lighted pathway leading from the beach to the resort and he glanced down at her. Silvery sand dusted almost every inch of her skin. Her hair had tumbled around her shoulders in a wild tangle of honey brown. The lower half of her dress was soaked from the surf, the upper half buttoned haphazardly. But it was the smile she flashed him that got Wolf so hard and tight again he almost doubled over.

If he worked at it, he could rationalize making love to her. He was almost ninety-nine-percent sure those were Cordell's goons out on that boat, listening in. By making an obvious show of taking Nina to bed, Wolf would mark her as his and send a signal to Cordell to back off.

It was that one percent that gnawed at him. So much, that his head was still waging a fierce battle with his body when the door closed behind them.

Nina had no such reservations. The moment they were inside she dropped her sandals, turned and tugged his shirt free of his slacks. With the tails came a shower of sand.

"We must have brought half the beach back with us," she said between quick, nipping kisses. "I hope we didn't bring anything else, Wo... Kevin."

She caught herself in time, but the near miss reinforced his decision to call a halt. Now. Before he let down his guard again and put her at even more risk.

"I'm sorry, Nina." He didn't have to feign a show of reluctance when he reached up and eased her arms from around his neck. "You were right earlier."

Confusion worked its way through the hot desire in her eyes. "About...?"

"I came down to Cabo thinking all I had to do was finesse you into bed to make things right between us. I see now that's not the way to win you back."

He had to touch her, if for no other reason than to blunt her dawning comprehension and dismay. He brushed a knuckle over her cheek and gave a small, almost imperceptible nod toward the flat screen TV.

"I still want you." God, he wanted her! "I'm willing to wait until you trust me again, though."

"You are, huh?" Shooting daggers at him, she played to their unseen audience. "We've got a long way to go before that happens, *Kevin*."

"I know."

"I'm glad you recognize that." She tossed her tangled hair and left him to stew in his own juices. "You know where the spare pillows and blankets are. Good night."

She didn't exactly slam the bedroom door, but the solid thud spoke volumes. Wolf thought about following her to explain his sudden about-face. The fact that he was afraid to test his tenuous control took everything he knew about himself and turned it upside down.

With a smothered curse, he went to the kitchenette to make a pot of coffee. It was going to be a long night. Even longer now that the brown-eyed doc had tied him in knots!

He waited until 2:00 a.m. to make his move.

Moving silently on bare feet, Wolf cracked the bedroom door. Nina's steady breathing assured him she was out for the count. The sheets tangled around her hips and legs suggested she hadn't gone down without a fight.

Guilt and regret nagged at him as he retrieved his gear bag from the closet where he'd stashed it earlier. He'd had plenty of time in the past few hours to acknowledge how badly he'd handled the situation down on the beach.

He should have called a halt after the first kiss. He was supposed to be the trained agent, the one with the cool head and iron nerves. Instead, he'd let his body call the shots. Like some overeager teen fumbling around with his girlfriend in the backseat of his daddy's car, for God's sake! He suspected Nina would take a long time forgiving that bit of idiocy.

With a silent apology, he clicked the door shut and went into the bathroom. He emerged a few minutes later in the wet suit he wore so often in his work that it felt like a second skin. A waterproof waist pack held his phone and the kit he'd put together for situations like this one. He'd left his scuba gear and air tanks in the trunk of Mannie's car, but he wouldn't need them for this job. Not with the roundabout anchored so close to shore.

Before exiting the casita, Wolf rigged one of Mac's low-tech but extremely effective alarms. If anyone tried the door while he was gone, a siren-like wail would wake Nina and everyone else within a half-mile radius.

A murmur of subdued voices drifted from the adult pool, but the rest of the resort had shut down for the night. Still, Wolf avoided the elevators and stuck to the shadow of the stairs that wound down to the beach. Once there, he turned left, away from

the moon-washed stretch of shore he'd walked with
Nina. His goal this time was the protected cove
sheltering the resort's water sports marina—and
the pleasure craft riding at the ends of their anchor
chains. There were four. Two sailboats with their
sails furled, one cabin cruiser showing only its
safety lights, and the twenty-two-foot runabout.

Before going into the water, Wolf extracted a
camo stick from his waist pack. A few quick strokes
blackened his face and hands. Then he entered
the sea at an angle that would allow him to take
advantage of the strong undercurrents to carry him
toward the runabout.

Cutting through the dark water felt as natural
to Wolf as breathing. It should. He'd spent half his
life in this dimension. All those years of training
and experience as a naval underwater demolition
specialist had led naturally to a follow-on career
in the same field. It was a dangerous and highly
specialized profession, but one he and the men he
employed excelled at.

This was what he knew, what he did. Instead of
tiring, Wolf felt his strength and stamina build a
little more with each stroke. And with each clean,
silent stroke, the runabout got a little closer.

Even in the darkness he could see the boat
was new and well maintained. Its fiberglass hull

gleamed. Its eco-friendly, air-cooled electric engine would ensure it entree into marinas trending away from traditional gas-powered boats.

Admiring the boat's sleek lines, Wolf slipped under the water and swam submerged until the hull loomed directly ahead. He surfaced portside, nothing more than a shadow on the dark water, and listened intently. The only sounds he picked up were the wash of waves against the hull and the creak of the anchor chain as the runabout rode the low swells.

As silent as an eel, Wolf swam to the stern and hauled himself over the side so carefully the gunwale hardly rocked. He crouched in the deck well, listening, waiting, his gaze locked on the dim light that speared through the cabin's half-closed hatch. Only when he was satisfied that he'd come aboard undetected did he approach the cabin.

The two-man crew was inside. One snored loudly in the runabout's bunk. The other sat slumped over the built-in table next to the bank of navigational equipment, his head on his crossed arms and a set of earphones on the table beside him.

With a grim smile, Wolf eased into the cabin, reached into his waist pack for two plastic capsules and pinched them under each man's nose. One whiff of the colorless, nonlethal gas would keep them both out cold for a good hour.

He needed less than a fraction of that to find what he'd come looking for. A handwritten log sat next to the ship-to-shore radio. The watchers had made annotations indicating each time Wolf and Nina had entered and exited the casita since noon. Ditto the times they'd engaged in conversations.

Two separate log entries indicated a radio report to "base," the latest one just after midnight. Beside the last entry was a note relaying instructions from Señor Cordell to maintain their position.

Well, that answered that question. It also confirmed Wolf's guess that Cordell had Nina lined up in his sights as a potential mark. Dollar signs must have flashed in front of the bastard's eyes when he discovered Dr. Grant was leading the charge in medical data collection, analysis and exchange. The possibilities for profit—and fraud— probably had him salivating.

The unexpected arrival of Nina's fiancé would have thrown a monkey wrench into whatever tentative plans Cordell had formed for her. If so, the fact that Kevin was still relegated to the living room sofa must have put a smile on the snake's face. He'd be eating that grin before too long, Wolf vowed silently.

Still restless, he prowled the small cabin. On a hunch, he sat down in front of the runabout's marine navigation system. It was state of the art, like everything else on the craft. Housed in a waterproof, shockproof case with an IP66 rating that ensured it would withstand the heaviest seas, the system connected wirelessly via Bluetooth to a GPS, a wind meter, a knot log, and depth-sounder fish-finder. All viewable on a fifteen-inch touch screen LCD with a sunlight readable display, no less.

Damn, Wolf thought wryly. Stealing government secrets obviously paid better than retrieving them. Lusting for a system like this one, he fingered the chart plotter icon and squinted at the long list that painted down the screen.

Another touch of the screen highlighted the three courses plotted in the past twenty-four hours. As each came up, Wolf studied them intently. The first charted the runabout's course from Sebastian Cordell's seaside villa to the Mayan Princess. The second would take the runabout home again.

The third, he saw with a leap of excitement, integrated the weather forecast and tides for 11:00 p.m. Thursday. This course led to a point off the tip of the Baja peninsula some seventeen nautical miles out to sea.

Cordell had invited Nina and Wolf for a short cruise on Thursday afternoon before he took his yacht out for a longer voyage that evening. Made sense that he'd have the runabout shadow the yacht and stay within hailing distance. Just in case.

Reenergized, Wolf went into the water and swam back to shore with clean, strong strokes. His phone came out the moment he cleared the surf.

"Yo, Wolfman. You're up early."

"So are you, Ace. Any news?"

"It's going down just as we anticipated. Cordell received a final bid for the merchandise just before his midnight deadline."

"Did he accept it?"

"Negative. But he did contact your pal, Alekseev, right after that call to advise him the bidding had closed. Alekseev wanted to know when he would designate a time and place for delivery."

"I think I know the time and place."

"No kidding?"

"No kidding. D-day is Thursday. H-hour is twenty-three hundred local, give or take."

"And the coordinates?"

Wolf relayed them, then waited while Ace pulled the location up on the control center's wall-size digital map.

"Looks like Cordell intends to make the exchange outside Mexico's territorial waters."

"Looks like. Mannie will want in on the take-down, though."

"Not a problem. I'll work the coordination at this end. We'll put eyes in the skies, buddy, and have an assault team hovering just over the horizon. What else can I do for you?"

"Arrange an extraction for Nina—Dr. Grant—before the assault Thursday evening. I want her safe and out of the picture."

"Roger that. I may just fly down there and extract her myself. I'm getting saddle sores from all this sitting around. I need some action."

Wolf's reaction was instant and visceral. He knew damn well that Ace's code name didn't refer solely to his ability to throw a jet around the sky at Mach 2. The cocky pilot scored as many hits on the ground as he did in the air.

"Fly down if you want," Wolf told his friend, "but understand this. Dr. Grant is off-limits."

His controller didn't pretend to misunderstand. A low whistle drifted through the phone.

"Like that, is it, Seabiscuit?"

"Yeah, Flyboy, it's like that."

It was most definitely like that.

The realization shook Wolf. It also made him

feel as predatory and territorial as the gray wolves re-introduced into Yellowstone National Park the last summer he worked there. He was just a kid. A long, lanky seventeen-year old about to enter his senior year.

Controversy over the proposed plan had been raging forever. Despite years of objections and a series of lawsuits by ranchers and hunters, the U.S. Fish and Wildlife Service finally brought in thirty-three breeding pairs to counter the out-of-control elk population. Wolf had never forgotten his first glimpse of the animals in their acclimation pens a few days before they were released into the wild. Those bared fangs and black, quivering gums made an indelible impression on a seventeen-year-old kid. So indelible, he had no trouble choosing a code name when he signed on with OMEGA.

Of course, Ace would tell it differently. *He* claimed Rafe had earned his handle by cutting love 'em and leave 'em women out of the pack, then doing precisely that.

Wolf should have listened to his instincts when they warned him Dr. Nina Grant wasn't the love 'em and leave 'em type. In less than forty-eight hours she'd gotten under his skin more than any woman he'd ever known. It wasn't just lust, although the prospect of sliding into bed and losing himself in her severely impacted his ability to walk upright.

The truth broadsided him while he made his way back to the pyramid illuminated dramatically against the night sky. For the first time in his life he wanted more than casual sex.

Damn if he didn't feel the most ridiculous need to brush the soft brown hair back from her cheek and nuzzle the skin behind her ear. To chuckle at her grimace when he laid that Pumpkin tag on her. Hear her gasp with surprise and delight as the surf swirled around her ankles.

He'd like to see her in her own world, too. She had to be one savvy business exec, more than able to hold her own in the boardroom. Throw in her expertise in the area of biomedical systems...

Wolf jerked to a halt in the shadow of a leafy jacaranda, as disgusted with himself as he was disconcerted. Christ! He had it bad. Much worse than he thought. Good thing he'd arranged to get Nina out of Cabo. He needed a clear head and the absolute assurance she was safe when he faced down Cordell and/or Alekseev.

He'd get her out now, he thought grimly, if he didn't need to maintain cover until Thursday. After that all bets were off.

Chapter 9

Nina woke Wednesday morning feeling sluggish and disgruntled and bitchy as hell.

Part of her pissy mood she could blame on the heat pouring through the sliding glass doors she'd left open last night. With the screen latched and the fan turning lazily overhead, she'd counted on the sea breeze and the murmur of the waves to help her get over being left high and dry by a certain rat fink undercover agent.

The ploy didn't work. Sticky with sweat, she rolled out of bed almost as uptight as when she'd flopped into it.

"Some vacation," she said, grousing to the

tangle-haired woman in the mirror before she padded across the room to close the sliding glass doors and flip on the air conditioning.

The sound of the shower going full blast didn't improve her mood. She urgently had to use the bathroom.

Still grousing, she went into the kitchenette and dumped the cold dregs from the coffee pot, then tapped an impatient foot while the fresh brew bubbled and her need to hit the bathroom mounted. Jaw set, she tried to think about what she would order for breakfast, about what she'd wear today, about *anything* except Rafe Blackstone wet and naked under those gushing jets.

That ploy didn't work either. Consequently, she greeted him with something less than friendliness when he finally emerged with a towel slung around his neck and his unsnapped jeans riding low on his hips.

"About time," she said, huffing. "I thought you were going to spend all day in there."

With a crooked smile, he zeroed right in on her problem. "Rough night?"

"Not at all. I slept like a baby."

Damn it! Why couldn't she lie better? She could feel her cheeks heating even as his smile took a wry twist.

"Sure glad someone did."

She started to remind him that sleeping on the couch was his idea, but settled for an airy wave in the direction of the kitchen. "I made a fresh pot of coffee. Help yourself while I hit the bathroom."

One more day, she reminded herself, as she twisted the jets to full power. Two at the most. That's all she and Wolf had to get through before they ended this farce.

After last night, the end couldn't come soon enough for Nina. She'd thought Kevin had put her through the mother of all emotional upheavals. This was fifty times worse. At least her former fiancé hadn't left her so sexually frustrated she wanted to hurl a lamp at his head.

Still simmering, she toweled off and clamped her wet hair on top of her head before examining the meager contents of the bedroom closet. There wasn't much to choose from. She hadn't packed for cruises with smarmy expatriates or lounging around with fake fiancés.

Since Wolf was in jeans, she went with white slacks, a turquoise T-shirt and a pair of flip-flops. Her soles slapped the tiles as she marched into the living room.

"What's on the agenda today?"

He hiked a brow at her tone, but shrugged and

handed her a fresh cup of coffee. "This is your vacation. I'm just along for the ride. What are you up for, Pumpkin?"

Enough was enough.

"Grinding your head into the sand if you call me that again. You know I hate it, *Kevin.*"

"Right. Sorry." He looked anything but contrite as he leaned his hips against the kitchen counter. "What do you want to do today?"

She knew several things she *didn't* want to do. Floating hip to hip in the pool for one. Sipping Champagne under a starlit sky for another.

"Let's start with breakfast," she said, sounding tart even to her own ears. "We can decide what to do or where to go from there."

When they stepped into the elevator that would zing them up to the main section of the resort, Rafe tried to soothe her ruffled feathers.

"I need to explain about last night."

"No explanations necessary." Chin held high, she stared straight ahead. "I got the message."

"Not the message I intended to convey."

"Really?" She turned and slid her sunglasses down to the tip of her nose. "You'd better clue me in then. I obviously misinterpreted those hot-and-heavy kisses down on the beach."

"No, that part was real enough."

"So, which part wasn't? The part where we hustled back to the resort? Or the part where you backed away like a frightened virgin?"

Wolf couldn't help it. He had to laugh, even though he knew Nina would take it the wrong way. Which of course she did.

"You think last night was funny?" she fumed.

"Not hardly. It's just—"

"What?" she demanded when he tried unsuccessfully to smother another chuckle.

"I've been accused of a lot of things over the years, but this is the first time anyone's ever thrown 'frightened' and 'virgin' at me in the same sentence."

Her mouth opened then snapped shut again.

"Okay," she said after a silence. "I'll concede that being nervous about your ability to perform last night may not have been the issue."

"Thanks."

"Then what was?"

His grin fading, Wolf tucked a loose strand behind her ear. The truth was harder to admit than he would have thought possible two days ago.

"Okay, here's the problem in a nutshell. I almost forgot where we were last night. Worse, I came close to forgetting the situation I've dragged you into."

Nina scowled, but before she could reply the elevator glided to a halt at the resort's terraced café.

"We're not done with this conversation," she warned before she stepped out.

Wolf suspected as much, and used the time that it took the hostess to show them to a table by the window and a waitress to supply them with a pot of coffee to gather his thoughts.

"I'm sorry," he said quietly. "Last night was all my fault. I shouldn't have let things get so out of hand down there on the beach."

"*Let* them get out of hand?" She sat back, studying him with another frown. "Are you usually so in control that you can turn your feelings on and off?"

Pretty much, Wolf admitted silently. *Until last night.*

"I dragged you into this mess," he reminded her. "It's my responsibility to get you out again safely. To do that I need to stay focused."

"Focused," she echoed stiffly as she buried her face behind the menu. "Right."

Hell! He was handling this all wrong. Wolf tried another tack.

"Listen to me, Pum…Nina. I don't want you hurt. If it wouldn't rouse Cordell's suspicions, I'd put you on a plane out of Cabo this morning. I may yet, if the situation gets any dicier."

The menu came down again and hit the table with a silverware-rattling thud.

"Now you listen to me. I'm in this as deep as you are. More to the point, I make my own decisions."

"Granted, but—"

"No buts." Temper flaring in her brown eyes, she leaned forward and stabbed the air with a forefinger for emphasis. "Get this straight, Blackstone. You are not 'putting' me anywhere."

She jerked the menu up again, leaving Wolf to contemplate the gold-embossed Mayan pyramid on its front cover…along with the possibility he might have to break another capsule, hold it under Dr. Grant's nose and call in Ace to make the extraction after all.

They spent the rest of the morning in what Nina would term a state of armed neutrality.

Conditions started to thaw when they went up for a late lunch. Nina found it difficult to remain hostile to a man with Rafe's quick, slashing grin and complete imperviousness to her snubs.

By early afternoon, she was ready to declare a truce. Especially since Rafe had cranked up her iPod and made several trips out to the balcony to take or return calls on his juiced-up phone. Each time he came back in, his leashed tension was almost palpable.

The call he'd obviously been waiting for came a little past three. He beckoned Nina out to the balcony and broke the news while she sat on the edge of the hot tub and swirled her feet in the bubbling water.

"Cordell's accepted the Russians' bid for his merchandise."

She shook her head in disgust. "How much is he getting to sell out his country?"

"Six million. Half to be wired to his account by the close of business today, the rest when he makes delivery."

"Which you think he's going to do by boat? Tomorrow? Somewhere off the Baja coast?"

"That's our best guess. We'll know for certain soon enough. Cordell told the Russians he would let them know when and where to rendezvous. If he sets up an exchange at sea, they'll need time to charter a boat and crew."

Nina shook her head in disbelief. Less than a week ago work had constituted her whole world. She went in to the office at 5:00 or 6:00 a.m. and didn't leave until late in the evening. The long hours and thrill of bringing in major new customers for her company's medical trending data had gone a long way toward blunting the sting of Kevin's betrayal.

Now here she was, sitting on the balcony of her luxurious casita, looking out over the sparkling blue Pacific. With this sexy hunk standing just a few feet away, no less. And instead of enjoying the view—or each other—they were calmly discussing a traitorous act of piracy that had already led directly or indirectly to the death of a United States senator.

"I don't understand why they're rendezvousing at all," she said, struggling to wrap her mind around the bizarre situation. "Why doesn't Cordell just transfer his 'merchandise' electronically?"

"The disk that disappeared from Senator Dewitt's office is encrypted. Its contents can't be copied or e-mailed."

"If it's encrypted, wouldn't Cordell need a special password or code to access it?"

"We have to assume he got the code from Senator DeWitt. Otherwise he'd have nothing to sell."

Ouch! That hit a little too close to home.

Before the Kevin fiasco, Nina would have scoffed at the idea of Sebastian Cordell duping a smart, savvy woman like Joyce DeWitt into allowing him access to highly classified technology. Now she felt only sympathy for the woman.

"Our boy is now in a classic standoff," Wolf said with a predatory smile. "He can't let the merchandise out of his hands until he sees the final payment, but he doesn't receive that payment until the customer sees the merchandise."

Nina shifted her gaze to the shimmering Pacific. Incredible to think Sebastian Cordell planned to take them aboard his gleaming yacht for the promised cruise along the Baja Peninsula a few hours before setting out on a far more dangerous voyage.

The silver-maned traitor had nerves of steel. She had to give him that. Not many men could play the gracious host simply to kill some time before rendezvousing with a badass lieutenant in the Russian mafia.

No, not simply to kill some time. If Wolf was right, Cordell had her lined up as a potential mark. The prospect gave Nina a creepy feeling that crawled along her nerves more with each passing hour.

Sheer desperation finally prompted her to suggest a temporary distraction. She waylaid Wolf in the living room and was careful to play for Cordell's listeners.

"You haven't seen much of Cabo San Lucas yet,

Kevin. Why don't we walk around town, then have an early dinner at the marina?"

"Sounds good," he replied, his eyes glinting. "One of the waiters at the pool yesterday mentioned a great place for margaritas and shrimp fajitas. The Pink Parrot, or something like that."

Incredible. She was a twittering bundle of nerves, and he was yanking her chain.

"I saw that place when I was downtown," she tossed back. "The parrot's purple, not pink."

"Whatever. I'd better slather another layer of sunscreen on you first. The backs of your legs are looking a little red." He scooped the lotion off the coffee table. "Turn around."

"I'll do it."

She snatched the lotion out of his hand and backed away. No way she was letting him slide his hands between her thighs again.

Duly slathered and smelling strongly of coconut, she called to have the rental car delivered from the parking area. The cheerful, smiling parking valet had it idling at the curb when they emerged from the open air lobby.

"*Buenos dias,* Dr. Grant, Señor James."

"*Buenos dias,* Ramon."

"I'd better drive," Wolf said as they approached the vehicle.

He'd taken the wheel of the rental before his too-casual comment registered with Nina.

"Why do you need to drive?"

"I know the town better than you do."

Also too casual. As he adjusted the rearview mirror, she bit her lip and wondered if she'd made a mistake by suggesting they get out for a few hours.

She got her answer less than thirty minutes later.

They'd just parked the rental and were strolling through the plaza in Cabo's open-air mall. A gallery with arched windows showcasing exquisitely painted pottery caught Nina's gaze, but Wolf spotted something entirely different in the windows.

"Hell!"

She glanced up and saw he'd locked on a wavy image reflected in the window. It showed the shop across the plaza, with two men standing just outside the front entrance.

Nina threw a startled glance over her shoulder. She had time to note only sketchy details—the shop was a tobacco store and the taller of the two men was rolling a fat black cigar between his thumb and forefinger—before Wolf thrust her at the gallery entrance.

"Get inside! Now!"

Her heart pounding, she reached for the elaborate brass latch and stumbled over the threshold.

"Who is it?" she asked when Wolf whipped in behind her.

"I don't know the one on the left. The tall one on the right is the Albanian sewer rat who pumped two rounds into me before I shot him."

"Please tell me you're kidding!"

"I wish."

Wolf used the pottery display as a screen and kept his eyes on the men across the plaza. "The hits must have thrown off my aim," he muttered in disgust. "I was sure I put one dead center before the whole friggin' warehouse blew."

"Your sewer rat," Nina gasped. "Do you think he's working for the Russians?"

"That would be my guess. Alekseev is probably inside the tobacco shop now, stocking up on hand-rolled Hobanas."

Albanians. Russians. Lying, stealing, scum-sucking Americans. The whole alternate universe thing was now officially freaking Nina out!

Scarcely able to breath, she peeked around Wolf. Her chest cramped when she spotted the taller of the two men frozen in place, staring at the gallery entrance. The cramp doubled in intensity when he said something to his pal and they started across the plaza.

"May I help you?"

The polite query almost brought Nina out of her skin. Close to hyperventilating, she slewed around to face a smiling salesperson.

"No, uh, thanks. We're just, um, looking."

She'd barely gasped out the reply before Wolf wrapped a hand around her upper arm. Hustling her past the startled saleswoman, he hauled her toward the rear of the gallery.

"Señor! You cannot go out that way!"

He ignored the woman's shout and hit the emergency release bar on the back door. The action triggered an ear-splitting alarm. Wincing, Nina hunched her shoulders against the vicious assault. She winced again when she caught a whiff of the garbage bins that lined the back alley, their contents steaming in the heat.

Wolf didn't give her time to adjust to the screaming siren or the stink. He shoved the rental's keys into her hand and rapped out instructions.

"Take the car. Drive straight back to the resort. Don't open the door for anyone except me or Mannie. Or Ace, my controller," he reminded her as he hiked up his pant leg. Ripping up the Velcro strap on his ankle holster, he straightened again in one fluid move.

"Wolf! What are you—"

"Go, Nina."

He spun her toward the north end of the alleyway and shoved. She took a few stumbling steps, then started to run.

Instinct told her she would only get in his way if she didn't do as he instructed. Or force him to take stupid risks to protect her. Or...

Oh, God!

She skidded to a stop and ducked behind a garbage can. One glance back down the alley twisted her insides in knots. Wolf stood at the far end of the alley. Clearly silhouetted against a bright shaft of sunlight, Nina saw as terror closed her throat.

He'd set himself up as a target to give her time to get away!

She wanted to scream at him to take cover, but she knew he wouldn't hear her over the screeching alarm. Then the sewer rat and his friend burst through the gallery's back door and she realized in a blinding flash that they couldn't hear her, either. Not with their entire attention fixed on the figure at the far entrance to the dank passageway.

Careful, precise, cautious Nina didn't stop to think. Snatching a lid off the garbage can, she charged down the alley.

Chapter 10

"She took the Albanian down with the lid from a *garbage can?*"

The stunned response coming through Wolf's cell phone might have made him grin if he wasn't still trying to recover. Even now, almost an hour after the fact, the image of Nina tearing down the alleyway had him leaning an elbow against the wall outside Mannie's office for support.

"She came at him from behind," he confirmed, "and whacked the hell out of him."

"Are you sure we're talking about the same woman?" Ace asked incredulously. "Isn't this the one who was so twittery and nervous about wearing a bug that you had to jump into the picture as her fiancé?"

"That's the one."

"Damn!"

"Yeah," Wolf drawled, "that was pretty much my reaction, too."

"Wait until I tell Lightning about this," Ace said, his voice filled with unholy glee. "One of OMEGA's crack agents creases the Albanian's skull in Paris a few years ago, and he walks away. Dr. Grant whacks him with the lid from a garbage can and he goes down for the count."

"Can we get serious here?"

"Sorry, Wolfman. You said two men came after you. I assume you took care of the second."

"I did. Mannie's got them both in holding cells. They're not talking, and he's not letting them make any calls. For the time being, anyway."

Wolf shifted just enough to peer inside the office Mannie and his elite federal task force had commandeered in Cabo San Lucas's central police station. Nina sat on the edge of a battered desk, her eyes huge, as Wolf's counterpart for this op regaled her with God knew what stories from their checkered past.

"What about their boss?" Ace wanted to know, reclaiming Wolf's attention.

"Alekseev was in a tobacco store across the plaza. Mannie's people grilled the shop owner. He swears he and his customer didn't hear the alarm go off in the alley behind the gallery, but realized something had happened when the police arrived on the plaza with sirens screaming. Reportedly, Alekseev rushed to the front entrance, saw his two watchdogs had gone missing, then cursed and tore back through the shop."

"So the Russian doesn't know what went down?"

"Not yet. He's got sources. He'll find out eventually. So will Cordell. The question now is whether this will spook them into calling off the deal."

The possibility ate at Wolf like battery acid. They were so close to nailing the traitorous bastard. So damn close. He hated the possibility they'd have to reinitiate surveillance and start all over again.

"My guess is they'll press ahead," Ace said. "The wire transfer for the first three million went through a half hour ago."

That should have been enough to take Cordell down. If the man hadn't been so careful, if he'd made an actual reference to the stolen technology during his so-called negotiations, Wolf and Mannie could move on him now. But all they had on tape were vague references to "merchandise." They had to nail him with the disk in his possession. Preferably at the time of hand-off, so they could catch the buyers in the same net.

Which would have happened tomorrow night, some seventeen miles out to sea.

Wolf gripped the phone in a white-knuckled fist. Every job he did for OMEGA involved uncertainties. The unexpected had to be anticipated. Things could—and often did—go wrong. He suspected that in other circumstances he would have assessed the implications of his encounter with the Albanian, calculated the risks and pressed ahead with the op as originally planned.

A sudden outburst of laughter brought Wolf around again. Nina had her head and shoulders back, chortling in delight. Despite her present merriment, she displayed ample evidence of their grim back-alley confrontation. The hair that spilled over her shoulders was damp with sweat. Dirt streaked one cheek. A variety of stains discolored her once-pristine white pants.

Slammed once again with the mental image of her charging down the alley, swinging that damn lid, Wolf opted instantly for Plan B.

"I want Dr. Grant out of Cabo this evening. Although we have the Albanian and his pal on ice,

I can't take the chance they'll get word to Alekseev, or tip Cordell to the fact that I'm not really her fiancé."

Ace had spent too many years in the field to question an operative's on-scene assessment. "Your call, Wolfman. I can set up an extraction and have her out of there in an hour."

"Make it two. There's a chance Cordell won't connect her—or me—to the incident with Alekseev's boys, so we need to make her departure look legit. I'll drive her back to the resort to pack her things and check out. That way, when she calls Cordell to tell him there's been an emergency at home and she has to leave Mexico, the hotel can verify that she's checked out and departed."

"Two hours works perfectly," Ace replied. "Diamond's in Scottsdale at a showing of her new line. T.J.'s with her. I'll set up a private jet and have one of them in Cabo by the time you get Dr. Grant to the airport."

Wolf felt the tight knot of tension at the base of his skull ease a fraction. Jordan Colby, code name Diamond, designed a line of high-fashion eyeware coveted by queens and teenagers alike. Only a few insiders knew that she donated all proceeds from her business to charities that cared for abused or abandoned children.

In her other life, Diamond was the one of the coolest agents under fire Wolf had ever worked with. Her husband, former NYC cop, T. J. Scott, was no slouch, either. T.J. could talk down, stare down or take down all comers. Wolf could trust either of them to keep Nina safe until he tied things up at this end and rejoined her.

Whoa! Where had that come from?

Until this moment, he hadn't thought beyond nailing Cordell and recovering the stolen technology. Now he was projecting ahead to more days with Nina. And nights. Like last night, he thought, with a sudden tightening in his belly, but with a *very* different ending.

Wolf waited until they were in the rental car and headed back to the Mayan Princess to inform Nina about the change in plans.

"The encounter with the Albanian upped the stakes." He kept an eye on the rearview mirror, as much from instinct as from nerves. "Mannie's promised to hold him incommunicado for the next twenty-four hours."

"Until after the exchange."

"Right. But there's no guarantee Alekseev won't nose out what happened, maybe finger me as the agent who tangled with his boy in Paris a few years back. If he does, he'll want to know what I was doing at Cordell's hacienda with you."

"Cordell will want to know the same thing," she said, with a catch in her voice. "This just keeps getting hairier and hairier."

"Which is why we need to get you out of it. This evening, Nina."

He braced himself for a spurt of angry protests. She'd made her feelings about staying in the game clear enough at breakfast. And he had to admit she'd more than held her own back there in the alley. To Wolf's surprise, she merely gave a small nod.

He should have let it go at that. He'd made his point. Had her unspoken acquiescence. No need to muddy the waters with a fumbling explanation.

"It's not just your confrontation with the Albanian," he heard himself say. "It's how I felt when I saw you charging down the alley."

That caught her attention. She cocked her head and studied him with an arrested expression. "How did you feel?"

Wolf hesitated. This was tougher than he'd imagined. He'd never told a woman he loved her before. He couldn't tell this one, either. The standard, hackneyed phrases just wouldn't come.

"Like the ground dropped out from under my feet."

"I felt pretty much the same way when I realized you were setting yourself up as a target to lead your Albanian pal away from me," she said slowly.

Wolf shot her a quick glance. So she'd tumbled to that, had she? He'd figured she'd just reacted instinctively back there in the alley. The realization that she'd put herself in the line of fire to save *him* reinforced Wolf's decision to get her out of Cabo.

"Then you understand why I need to know you're safe, Pumpkin. Otherwise I won't be able to concentrate on my job, and that doubles the risk to both of us."

Nina understood all right. She didn't like it, but she understood.

These days and nights with Rafe Blackstone had triggered something inside her. Some craving for adventure and excitement she'd never realized she possessed. It was as though he'd flicked a switch and turned on a hidden Nina. Bolder, braver, more reckless.

Everything in her resisted the idea of flicking the switch to Off again and going back to her safe, secure world. But the possibility that her continued presence in Cabo could get Wolf killed overrode every other consideration.

She took heart from the unspoken message buried in his gruff admission, however. Even more from that ridiculous nickname. Suddenly being compared to a slice of Thanksgiving pie didn't seem quite as obnoxious as it had before.

"Don't worry," she told him. "I'll go quietly, sheriff."

The smile he flashed her almost made up for being hustled out of Cabo. Almost.

"Here's the deal. Ace is sending a private jet to pick you up, along with another OMEGA agent to act as your escort. She, or he, will stay with you until this op terminates and I can join you in Albuquerque."

Nothing hidden in that message! The excitement started to trickle back.

"You're coming to Albuquerque?"

"That's the plan." He slanted her an inquiring glance. "Unless you say otherwise."

Was he kidding? Delight curled in her belly, but she was darned if she'd make it that easy for him.

"So now I get a vote?"

His smile turned wicked. "Not really. I was just being polite. You and I have some unfinished business to take care of, Dr. Grant."

She wanted to follow up on that interesting comment, but Wolf insisted they use the remaining five or ten minutes until they reached the casita to rehearse the exit lines they'd feed to Cordell's listeners.

They assumed their respective roles as soon as he'd keyed the front door and done a quick sweep of the interior. Ushering Nina inside, he tossed the key card on the counter and did his best to project a disgruntled lover.

"I can't believe your biggest customer calls you and insists he *has* to meet with you tomorrow morning. This is your first vacation in years. What's so serious it can't wait until next week?"

"I told you. Mike has a good shot at fifteen million in medical-reform dollars. He needs sanitized data from us, like yesterday, to demonstrate the viability of the med-chip he proposes to imbed under patients' skin."

"Well at least he's sending his private jet for us. Sure hate to miss going out on your friend Cordell's boat, though. You'd better call him and cancel."

"I'll do that right now."

Much to Nina's relief, Cordell's answering machine clicked on. She might have discovered a newfound bravado in herself, but she was still the world's worst liar.

"Hi, Sebastian. This is Nina Grant. I'm so sorry,

but Kevin and I have to bow out of the cruise tomorrow afternoon. Something's come up at work and I need to get back to Albuquerque. We're flying home in a few hours."

She had to force herself to fumble through her last few lines.

"I, uh, enjoyed meeting you. I hope I'll see you again sometime."

Like in the newspapers, when she read that he'd been sentenced to ten to twenty years.

"Thanks again for your hospitality."

Despite her newfound craving for excitement, she felt only a sense of relief when she hung up. This undercover business did a real job on the nerves.

"Need help getting packed?" Wolf asked casually.

"No thanks. I'm good. Or maybe not," she amended as he followed her into the bedroom.

She thought he wanted to add some last-minute instructions or make sure she gathered all her belongings. She did *not* expect him to shut the door, catch her arm and spin her against the wall.

"About that unfinished business…"

Her breath caught. "Yes?"

He planted an arm beside her head and smiled down at her. Nina could see herself reflected in his eyes. She saw something else as well. Something that made her heart thud against her ribs.

"I thought maybe you should take this home with you."

"This" was a slow, sensual kiss. An erotic blend of touch and taste and tongue.

Slow was good. Great, in fact. But Nina needed more. Hooking her arms around his neck, she made that abundantly clear. Her mouth locked on to his. Angling, she canted her hips into his lower body. The effect was instantaneous and everything she'd hoped for.

With a low grunt, Wolf wrapped an arm around her waist and pulled her against him. His kiss got harder, hotter. So did Nina. Consumed by the searing heat, she fanned the flames even more by hooking an ankle around his calf and grinding her hips into his. She could feel him harden, thicken, until his entire length pushed at her through the zipper of his jeans.

"How…?" She jerked her head back, gasping. "How long before we have to leave for the airport?"

He stared down at her, his blue eyes smoky. He wanted more, too, she saw on a wave of reckless exhilaration.

"How long, Wolf?"

A muscle ticked in his jaw. He didn't answer for five seconds, ten. Nina was ready to drag him bodily to the bed when he growled down at her.

"Long enough."

The first time was frenzied. Frantic. Right there, against the wall.

She tore at the buttons of his shirt and ripped it down his arms, needing to touch him, taste him. He shed the shirt without breaking contact. His mouth was locked on hers and his hands rough as he hiked up her T-shirt. She had to pull away to get it over her head.

That gave Wolf the perfect opening. Contorting, he dropped nipping kisses across the slopes of her breasts. By the time she shimmied out of her bra, he'd tugged down her slacks and had a hand between her thighs.

She was ready for him—hot and wet and so ready she almost came right then. But when he yanked down her briefs, safe, cautious Nina surfaced with a small shriek.

"Wolf! Please tell me you've got a condom in your wallet!"

"Sorry, sweetheart."

She groaned, and he grinned.

"But I do have several in my gear bag. Don't move. Do *not* move!"

"Like I could?"

She splayed both hands against the plaster and almost quivered with need. Wolf wasn't in much better shape. He'd never wanted any woman as badly as he did this one. Hunger for her burned in his belly, so fierce and primitive it took him three tries to tear open the damn condom.

The delay was brief, only a few seconds. Just long enough for a thin thread of sanity to snake through the red haze in his head. He'd called a halt last night to keep from losing his focus. The situation hadn't changed. If anything, it had grown more serious. What was he doing, slamming Nina up against the wall and going at her like some drunken sailor?

He turned with the condom in his hand. His second thoughts must have shown in his face, because Nina drew in a swift breath, reached out and hooked a hand in his waistband.

"Oh no," she breathed, hauling him against her. "Not this time, Blackstone."

Their second round lasted longer. Probably because their first orgasm was so explosive Wolf had to brace one hand against the wall and hold

Nina up with the other while his chest heaved and the blood slowly returned to his extremities. Or maybe because he wanted to explore the curves and hollows he'd missed the first time around.

Whatever the reason, he took sensual delight in leading her to the king-size bed. She arched like a cat on the clean sheets, one arm over her head, a smile curving her lips.

"Again?"

"Again," he replied, with a grin. "As soon as I get my wind back. In the meantime…"

He stretched out beside her and propped his head on a hand. The other he skimmed over her belly and breasts. The damp, silky texture of her skin combined with the yeasty scent of their lovemaking to get him hard again. Much quicker than Wolf would have believed possible.

Despite the sudden rush of blood and the clock ticking away at the back of his mind he forced a deliberation he was far from feeling. He made every kiss a new discovery, each touch a sensual invitation.

Nina responded slowly at first. Limp and languid, she let him explore at will. Gradually, her breathing quickened and the body he'd teased back to life took on a coiled tension that matched his own.

Wolf hated to end it but the damn clock kept

ticking. Burying his hands in her hair, he slid in, pulled back, thrust home. Her eyes flew open. Wolf looked down at them and knew he'd met the one woman who could change his world. Had changed his world. For the first time in all his years with OMEGA, his mission took second priority.

He should have told her then. Should have said the words that wanted to come so badly he had to bite them back.

Wolf *thought* he was doing the right thing by covering her mouth with his and thrusting in again. *Thought* he had all bases covered when Ace called to confirm that Diamond would touch down at the airport in a little less than thirty minutes. *Thought* all he had to do was hustle Nina aboard the private jet and finish his job down here in Cabo.

He should have known it wouldn't be that easy.

Chapter 11

The attack came on the way to the airport. Wolf spotted the car following them just moments after they'd pulled out of the Mayah Princess' long, curving drive.

"We've got company," he said with a glance in the rearview mirror.

"Again!"

With a weird sense of déjà vu, Nina twisted to peer out the back window. She'd dressed comfortably for travel in drawstring slacks and her red silk tank. They moved easily with her as she searched the early evening haze and tried to pick out their tail.

"Who do you think…?"

"Hell!"

Wolf's curse brought her slewing back around in time to see a Hummer shoot out of a side street and screech to a halt just yards ahead.

"Omigod!"

Yelping, Nina braced both arms on the dash. Wolf cursed again, stood on the brakes and fought the wheel. Their car made almost one-eighty before coming to a squealing, shuddering stop on the dirt shoulder.

The Hummer's passenger had leaped out before the rental's tires stopped spinning. Nina's stomach did a somersault when she recognized the same muscled-up thug who'd searched her bag the afternoon her car broke down. But before she could so much as shout a warning to Wolf, the man smashed her window with his gun butt and screwed the barrel into her temple.

"Señor Cordell wants to see you," he sneered. "You, too, gringo. Get out of the car slowly. Very slowly. Do not force me to blow your woman's brains all over you."

Nina couldn't flick Wolf even a single glance. The barrel jammed so brutally against her temple prevented her from turning her head. She heard a door snick open though, and saw his jean-clad leg swing out.

"Now you," Cordell's thug instructed.

The vicious pressure eased for a fraction of a second. Just long enough for him to yank open the car door, ram the barrel against Nina's neck, and haul her out onto the dirt shoulder. Silvers of broken glass fell from her lap like teardrops. Her sandals crunched on the shards as the muscle-bound creep propelled her toward the Hummer.

"Get in. And you, gringo."

Wolf didn't move. Nina could see him only out of the corner of one eye. That glimpse was enough to stop her heart. His face could have been carved from stone, but his eyes were lethal.

He was going to do something stupid! Make some ridiculously heroic self-sacrifice to save her!

"Just go along with them," she pleaded desperately. "Please!"

"You'd better listen to your woman, gringo."

A screech of tires underscored his warning. The car tailing them, Nina realized, as two more men jumped out and approached Wolf with guns in hand.

Other traffic whizzed by. She saw a shocked face or two pressed against a window, but no one stopped. She had time for only a short, fervent prayer that someone would call the police before Cordell's thug shoved her into the rear door of the Hummer.

Sprawled half-across the seat, she tried to push up. Then the driver reached back, clamped a hand on her neck and mashed her face into the leather.

"Hey!"

Half smothered, she barely felt the tiny prick in her bare arm. When she realized she'd been stuck, she bucked frantically. Every horror story she'd ever heard or read about contaminated needles and infectious diseases rose up to choke her. Fear consumed her as an icy heat raced from her arm to her neck to her chest.

"What...?" Her tongue felt thick. Her lungs had to fight to pull in air. "What did...you...give me?"

"Something to keep you quiet."

As if from a distance, she heard Wolf's vicious snarl.

"You filthy bastards!"

Something hit with a sickening crunch. Bone on bone? Steel on bone? Nina couldn't drag the answer from the gray mist swirling across her mind. She had one last, coherent thought before the mist closed in.

This can't be happening!

* * *

She came awake to the sour taste of bile.

Nausea churned in her stomach. The bed she was lying on rolled. The darkened room spun. A low, constant thump repeated over and over inside her head. Groaning, Nina squeezed her eyes shut again.

She woke a second time moments later. Or was it hours? She had no clue. Breathing through her nose, she tried desperately to control her queasy stomach while her eyes became accustomed to the gloom. She was in a bedroom, she saw. A large and very elegant bedroom, boasting teak built-ins, subdued lighting, and small, square windows curtained in straw-colored silk.

Frowning, Nina focused on the curtains. Were they swaying, or was she? They were *both* moving, she realized, when the bed dipped gently beneath her. She pushed up on one hand, shoved back her tangled hair with the other and took a closer look at her surroundings.

Okay. All right. She had the picture now. The bedroom was actually a luxuriously outfitted cabin. Aboard Sebastian Cordell's monster yacht, if those sculptures in recessed niches were any indication. The swaying—and the sound she now recognized as the gentle thump of waves against the hull—meant the boat was out to sea.

The realization produced a spurt of profound relief. Maybe, just maybe, the churning in her stomach wasn't a residual effect of whatever Sebastian's goons had given her. The biologist in her cringed at the thought that some unknown toxin might be lingering in her system. With any luck, she was just feeling incipient motion sickness.

She sat still for a moment, her legs dangling over the side of the bed, and tested her theory. Another slow roll confirmed it. Thank God! She could handle seasickness. She *had* to handle it.

Pushing off the silk coverlet, she thrust her feet into the sandals someone had aligned neatly beside the bed. She didn't see her tote or anything she could use as a weapon. Except...

Her jaw set, Nina marched over to one of the recessed niches and wrapped her fist around the neck of a slender marble nymph. The sculpture was either glued or plastered to its pedestal but came off after several hard tugs. She took a few experimental swings, deriving fierce satisfaction from the heavy weight of the nymph's base.

All right, Cordell, she thought, as she headed for the door. Prepare to meet one pissed woman.

She fully expected to find the door locked,

and almost fell through when it swung open on well-oiled hinges. Stumbling, she came face to face with an equally startled steward in a starched white jacket. He jumped back and barely avoided tipping his tray of crystal wine glasses.

"Hey!" Nina gasped. "I know you!"

"*Sí,* Dr. Grant. I am Enrique, Señor Cordell's chief steward. I served you drinks at his hacienda when you…*Madre de Dios!*"

His eyes widened with horror, and Nina swung around. She had the nymph hefted, ready to come crashing down on an attacker, when Enrique gasped out an urgent plea.

"That statue, Dr. Grant! It is one of Señor Cordell's most cherished. You must—"

"The man I was with," she interrupted fiercely, spinning back around. "My fiancé. Where is he?"

"With Señor Cordell in the main salon. I will take you there. But first," he entreated, "you will return the statute to its place, yes?"

"No way. Let's go."

He gave her another pleading look. Nina ignored it and kept the marble nymph at the ready as he edged past her. It stayed ready while she followed him down a wood-paneled corridor.

She couldn't quite believe he'd agreed to take her

to Sebastian so readily. Was it a ruse? Would one of Cordell's goons jump out of a side passageway when she passed and poke another needle in her arm? The very real possibility kept Nina so tense she forgot all about her propensity to upchuck every time she left dry land.

"Up here, Doctor."

Wine glasses tinkling, Enrique stood aside so she could precede him up a shallow flight of stairs. Nina gripped the statue in a white-knuckled fist and mounted the steps. She paused three stairs from the top to survey a room that seemed to stretch the entire length of the yacht.

The first thing she noticed were the floor-to-ceiling windows running half the length of the salon. On one side, the bank of windows showcased only pitch blackness. On the other, lights twinkled in the far distance. They were miles and miles off the coast, she realized with a gulp of dismay.

She took another hesitant step and saw that the vast salon included three different seating areas, each with its own entertainment center and flat screen TVs. Stock quotes scrolled across one, headline news across another. The third screen was blank. Probably because the two men seated across from each other on opposite sides of the TV had other matters on their mind than news or stock quotes.

So, apparently, did the man perched on a barstool in front of a gleaming teak bar. It was fitted with recessed lighting and railed shelves, with Cordell's two-thousand-dollar bottle of tequila holding the place of honor on the middle shelf. Nina barely registered the shell-shaped bottle. Her focus was all on the gun the individual at the bar held level and aimed at Wolf.

The gunman spotted her first and called out a soft warning. "Señor Cordell!"

Sebastian turned and when he saw Nina, he rose from his white leather captain's chair with every evidence of delight. Looking the essence of the nautical male in tan slacks, a navy blazer and white silk ascot, he held out a hand.

"So you're awake at last, my dear. We've been waiting for you. Please, come and join us."

She refused to take another step until Wolf added a gruff endorsement.

"It's okay. Come on up."

She guessed it was as far from okay as it could get, but mounted the last step anyway. Enrique followed and made for the bar with his tray of glasses. Sebastian, unbelievably, played the gracious host.

"I'm so pleased to see you up and about, my dear. You must be thirsty. Shall I pour you a drink?"

"No."

"Are you sure?"

When she simply stared at him stonily, he spread his hands in a graceful gesture.

"I really must apologize for the distress my men caused you. It was necessary, as I'm sure you'll agree when I…"

He broke off, his gaze dropping to the object gripped in her hand. His face took on the same horrified expression his steward's had a few moments ago.

"My dear! That's a priceless work of art you're wielding like a club."

"Is that so?"

"It's a Greek water naiad," he said with a touch of desperation, "sculpted by an unknown artist in the second century B.C."

"Yeah, well, this little naiad is going to hit the bulkhead in about two seconds if a certain twenty-first-century piece of slime doesn't order his friend at the bar to hand Wolf that gun."

She hoisted the statue, fully prepared to carry out what she knew in her heart was an empty threat.

"Nina! I implore you. That piece is irre-placeable."

And she and Wolf weren't? The implication made her ache to bring Cordell's nymph crashing down on his head.

"Destroying the statue will cause me considerable grief," he admitted, keeping a wary eye on his precious marble, "but I promise it will gain you nothing."

He'd called her bluff, damn it! She ought to smash the thing just for spite. She might yet, she thought, as she lowered her arm.

Cordell gave an audible sigh of relief. So did Enrique. Wine glasses rattling, the steward set the tray on the end of the bar.

"Thank you, Enrique." Recovering his poise, the master dismissed his servant. "We'll serve ourselves."

The white-jacketed steward avoided Nina's gaze as he passed her en route to the stairs.

"Thanks a lot," she muttered to his retreating back.

Skirting a cream-colored sofa, she moved to Wolf's side and got her first look at the ugly bruise on his right temple. So that bone-crunching thud she thought she'd heard hadn't been some drug-induced hallucination! Cordell's thugs had put Wolf to sleep the hard way.

Furious, she tightened her fist on the statue and

swung on Sebastian again. "You think you can get away with drugging and beating and kidnapping people?"

"I regret having to resort to such extremes, my dear. I prefer to avoid violence when possible but as you can see, my men had to take rather direct action with your friend here. I assure you, however, the agent they administered to you will leave no lasting effects."

"What was it, Sebastian? What did they inject me with?"

"Of course you would want to know. It's your profession, isn't it?"

The condescending comment made Nina seriously consider knocking his capped teeth down his throat.

"I have the mixture prepared at a lab in Dallas. It's extracted from castor beans and..."

"Ricin!" The sudden lurch her stomach made had nothing to do with the boat's motion. "You had your people pump ricin into my veins!"

"In a very small, very controlled amount, I assure you."

"I certainly hope so!"

The military had developed ricin for use in biological warfare. The toxic agent could be dispensed as a cloud, enveloping whole cities, and caused permanent paralysis if inhaled in significant quantities. Swallowed or injected, it could precipitate a slow, agonizing death.

The fact that she'd survived the injection substantiated Cordell's claim that she'd received a carefully calibrated dosage. Enough to incapacitate but not completely shut down all bodily functions. Still, the mere idea that she'd had the deadly toxin swimming through her veins made her throat go tight.

"I can't believe you would let your people play around with that stuff, much less inject it."

"Only into those who show up at my gates and gain entrance to my hacienda under false pretenses," Cordell returned. "Like you and the gentleman posing as your fiancé."

She threw Wolf a helpless glance, but tried to brazen it out. "Who says he's posing?"

"No need to continue the pretense, my dear. From what I read about your fiancé when I researched *you,* the real Kevin James isn't the type to strap a snub-nosed police special to his ankle."

She couldn't argue with that. Wolf didn't bother to try.

"Let's all cut the act, Cordell or Caulder or whatever the hell you want us to call you. Nina knows who you are. You know—or think you do—who I am. The only question left to answer is whether you'll make it easy on yourself and surrender voluntarily."

"And if I choose not to?" he inquired with silky menace.

The two men measured each other. Stripped of every semblance of civility, they emanated a dangerous aura that raised the hairs on the back of Nina's neck.

"You're going down, Cordell. One way or another."

"If I do, I'll take you and Dr. Grant with me."

The threat was real—*very* real, considering the gun still leveled at them by the man at the bar.

Gulping, Nina tightened her grip on the marble nymph. She'd played some sports in high school and college but would never claim to have much of a throwing arm. Maybe if she got closer…

She didn't have to feign a case of the jitters as she paced nervously. Her throat tight, she responded to Cordell's lethal promise to take her and Wolf down with him.

"Like you did Senator DeWitt?" she asked.

"Ah, yes. Beautiful, clever Janice." What looked like genuine regret crossed the man's face. "So tragic, her suicide, and so completely unnecessary."

"If it *was* suicide," Wolf countered grimly.

"It was, I assure you. I certainly had no reason to dispose of her. She gave me what I wanted."

"Let's talk about that, Cordell. You have to know we're not going to let you hand the disk you stole over to the Russians. Or anyone else, for that matter."

"Aren't you? Well, we'll see soon enough. Are you sure I can't pour either of you a drink? I brought the Azteca with me. We have time to indulge before Alekseev arrives."

Wolf didn't bat an eye, but Nina wasn't as skilled at masking her emotions. Cordell read her dismay like an open book.

"Yes, my dear. After the incident in the plaza this afternoon, the purchaser and I decided to move up delivery of the merchandise. We'll make the exchange tonight, not tomorrow night as planned. Then Sebastian Cordell will disappear, just as Stephen Caulder did. So, I'm afraid, will you and your companion."

Oh, God! Did Wolf's people know about the schedule change? Had he managed to get word to them, or to Mannie Diaz? Or the people who were supposed to have met her at the airport? They must have suspected the worst when she and Wolf didn't show. They had to be trying to locate them. If not…

Nausea churned in her stomach again. Swallowing hard, she forced herself to take a few more paces.

"I think I'll take that drink after all."

"Very good, my dear. Let's have the Azteca, shall we?"

Cordell went to the bar, taking care not to block his underling's line of fire. With great deliberation he lifted the shell-shaped bottle from its shelf.

"Alekseev was the one who tipped me to the incident in the plaza, by the way. He didn't have all the details. Only that a *Norte Americana* and her companion had tangled with two of his men."

He ran a fond glance over the spikes of the shell-shaped bottle. Almost like a lover admiring his mistress. Or, Nina thought with a sudden kick to her pulse, a man with a fortune in his hands.

"Alekseev was unable to speak with his men, but he did obtain a description of the American woman and her companion from the sales clerk who witnessed the event. When Alekseev relayed that description to me, I knew immediately it had to be you two."

Nina barely heard him. The medallion in the bottle's center had her full attention. She'd thought it was bronze when Cordell had flashed his precious Azteca in the bright sunlight, but the fluorescent lighting gave it a different hue. More slate colored, and smooth. Very smooth. Much like…

"Señor Cordell?"

The sudden appearance of a crewmember jerked Nina's attention away from the medallion.

"Yes?"

"We're approaching the rendezvous point."

Chapter 12

The rendezvous! Dear God!

Her heart in her throat, Nina whipped her horrified gaze from the crewman to Wolf. He'd pushed to his feet, his muscles coiled and his eyes dangerous.

"If he takes a single step," Cordell instructed the gun-toting henchman still seated at the bar, "shoot the woman."

The threat rooted Wolf to the polished teak flooring.

"Yes, I thought that would stop you," Cordell mused before giving Nina an appraising glance. "You're quite a surprise, my dear. When we first met, my instincts told me you were ripe for the plucking. The research I did on you confirmed those instincts. Even after you brought your so-called fiancé for a visit, I sensed a fire in you that had yet to be tapped. Now…"

"Now?" she echoed, her jaw tight.

"Now," he said with a knowing smile, "it appears our friend here has done some serious tapping."

She certainly couldn't argue with that. The stolen hour with Wolf before they'd left for the airport had rocked her world. In a blinding flash of insight, she knew that whatever happened in the *next* moments or hours, she'd tasted more of life and love with Rafe Blackstone during the past few days than she ever had before.

"You're quite magnificent," Cordell continued with mingled admiration and regret, "prepared to do battle for your man, armed only with my water naiad."

She'd forgotten all about the damn statue still clutched in her hand. It took everything she had not to fling it at Sebastian's head as he replaced his precious bottle of Azteca in its protective rack.

"I'm sorry, but I must ask you both to sit down and wait quietly while I greet my business associate."

With the small, round barrel aimed at her

midsection, Nina gave up all hope of getting close enough to disable the gunman. Sebastian sighed with audible relief when she retreated to the leather sectional. She eased down beside Wolf and placed the water nymph on the brass-trimmed coffee table.

"When my business is concluded," Sebastian promised, "we'll have our drink."

"You know what you can do with that drink."

Ignoring her sarcasm, he issued a final admonition to his henchman to keep a close eye on them and mounted the polished teak stairs to the upper deck. The tension he left behind was so thick that Nina jumped when Wolf covered her hand to give it a squeeze.

"That stuff Cordell's men pumped into you?" he asked in a murmur. "It didn't leave any residual effects?"

"Not that I can feel."

This is so surreal, she thought wildly, as she gripped Wolf's hand. Almost like an out-of-body experience. Here they were, ensconced on a cloud-soft leather sofa in a luxurious salon fit for a Saudi prince. With a gun pointed in their direction. After a murderous bastard calmly announced he intended to dispose of them. Yet Wolf's primary concern at the moment appeared to be her health.

Fighting a rising panic, Nina kept her voice low and one eye on their watchdog. "What's the plan? What're we going to do?"

"Sit tight, for the moment."

That wasn't exactly what she wanted to hear.

"What about your contacts? Mannie Diaz? The people who were supposed to meet us at the airport? Were you able to signal any of them?"

"No, but we've had Cordell under surveillance since the start of this op. They know what's happening."

"So why…?" She stopped and took a deep breath to contain the hysteria that threatened to spiral out of control. "So why aren't they here?"

"They will be."

His utter confidence should have reassured her. Unfortunately it contrasted dramatically with the lethal calculation that leapt into his eyes when the deck beneath their feet gave a delicate shudder and the boat began to slow.

Wolf ignored the grinding pain from the blow to his temple, ignored the tension that had been gnawing at his insides from the moment he'd come awake, ignored everything but the woman he'd dragged into this mess.

"Listen to me, Nina."

He'd been waiting for this moment. The crew

would be absorbed with maneuvering their luxury craft into position alongside whatever boat Alekseev had chartered. Cordell was on deck, overseeing operations.

"We don't have much time now. Here's what I want you to do. Jump up, cross your arms over your middle and act scared, real scared."

"*Act?*" she squeaked.

With another shudder, the yacht came to a dead stop. It was now or never.

"Jump up," Wolf murmured without showing any hint of the urgency knotting his gut. "Grab your middle, then keel over in a dead faint. Got that?"

"I…"

"Now, Pumpkin."

"Oh, God!"

The wild panic in her eyes when she lunged off the sofa was so vivid it startled even Wolf for a second. More to the point, it brought their watchdog's gun up with a jerk.

"I can't take this! I can't!"

Wolf rose as well and reached out as if to soothe her.

"No! Don't touch me! I'm—" she gripped her middle and bent over, moaning "—I'm going to be sick."

"Christ! She needs water," he snarled at their heavy-set guard. *"Agua!"*

Nina sank to her knees between the sofa and coffee table, retching with such realism that Wolf knew in that instant she wasn't acting. He angled his body between her and the guard and shouted over his shoulder.

"Agua!"

The guard hesitated for two or three agonizing seconds before sliding off his stool and moving behind the counter. As he yanked at the door of the bar fridge, his gun never wavered and his eyes didn't leave the two of them for a second. The only opportunity that arose, the only opportunity Wolf knew he'd get, came when the guard rounded the counter again and moved just close enough to toss a plastic water bottle across the intervening space.

He shoved Nina down with one hand. The other swept the marble nymph off the table. The statue passed the water bottle in midfight. It caught the guard right between the eyes before crashing to the deck and splintering into a hundred pieces.

Wolf came right behind it. He lunged low and fast as the guard stumbled back, firing wildly. The first shot whizzed past Wolf's ear and thudded into the bulkhead behind him. The second tore through his upper arm. He didn't feel the hit, never noticed the pain, as he slammed his fist into the man's face.

Bone crunched on bone. Blood spurted from the thug's pulped nose, adding to the torrent gushing from the cut in his forehead. His eyes rolled back in his head. With a strangled grunt, he slumped to the deck.

Wolf wrenched away the man's weapon and spun on one heel. "Let's go!"

"Go where?" Nina gasped, scrambling up from her crouch.

"Back to the fantail." He grabbed her arm to haul her with him. "I want you over the side and in the water before the real fireworks start."

"In the water?" Her feet dragged. "With sharks and barracuda and stingrays?"

"I'll put you in a launch." He listened for the thud of feet running on the deck above them. Cordell and company had to have heard the shots, had to be on their way...

Wolf broke off as the sounds he'd been expecting exploded. Footsteps pounded on the deck above. Shouts rang out. A scuffle sounded at the top of the forward stairs.

He shoved Nina toward the salon's aft exit. They catapulted into the narrow corridor bordered by staterooms and ran like hell. Behind them, a shrill, agonized cry rose above the general tumult.

"My naiad!"

With Nina in the lead, they rounded a corner and smacked into Cordell's white-coated steward. Enrique stumbled back, his eyes bugging, but before he could let out more than a gasp, Wolf clipped him with the gun butt. Enrique went down like a felled ox.

"This way."

Another turn, and they sprinted the last few yards to the stairs leading up to the aft lounge and deck. Nina was panting when they burst out onto the deck, with its sweeping views. As far as she could see, the Pacific undulated in shades of deep purple and the darkest green. Squinting, she made out faint lights in the distance.

Very faint lights!

In the *very* far distance!

"Wolf, I don't think…"

"Quiet!"

He thrust out an arm, shielding her behind him while he skimmed a quick glance along the yacht's starboard side. Nina peered over his shoulder and gulped when she spotted a deep-sea fishing boat tethered to Cordell's craft by mooring lines. Two individuals with obvious Slavic features stood with Uzis at the ready in the boat's open deck. The Russians had most definitely arrived!

"Over here."

Wolf propelled her toward the small launch hoisted on davits on the portside. She could hear men shouting below, doors slamming one after another. Cordell and his crew, checking the staterooms and galley, she guessed. Her heart in her throat, she watched while Wolf ripped off the launch's cover and released the winch to let it splash down into the sea. It bobbed just a few feet below the rail.

"Here you go," Wolf said urgently as he unlatched the rail gate.

She approached the opening, feeling ridiculously helpless. "I don't know how to start the engine."

With a muttered oath, he dropped into the launch and pumped a button a few times. When the engine kicked to life he held up a hand.

"Now, Nina."

She swallowed—hard—and stepped down. The small boat lurched under her feet.

Don't think about the motion!

Do not think about it!

Fighting fear and incipient nausea, she let Wolf position her at the wheel. He dropped a quick, hard kiss on her lips.

"Now go."

"Come with me," she begged.

Too late. He'd already swung back aboard. Her last sight of his broad back was as he raced over to the port side. To show himself to the Russians, she guessed, with a sick feeling in her heart, and direct pursuit away from her.

Only this time, she couldn't charge back to help him. She was puttering through dark, rolling swells in this friggin' boat. She could barely steer the thing, much less use it as battering ram.

Where were his friends? What were they waiting for? Why in hell didn't they...?

The answer to her frantic questions blazed out of the night with sudden, blinding potency. One after another, high-intensity spotlights stabbed through the darkness. Five. Eight. Ten or more! Completely surrounding the tethered yacht and fishing boat.

The spots came from rubber rafts, she saw before she threw up an arm to block the eye-searing glare. Small, silent rubber rafts that had come in under the yacht's sophisticated radars! With machine guns mounted in their bows! Blinded but gleeful, Nina did a mental happy dance while a voice blasted through a bullhorn.

"Ahoy! Yo soy teniente Escobar, Marina de Guerra de México. Estamos veniendo a bordo."

Her glee turned to acid in the next second. She was sure she would hear the stutter of machine gun fire, braced herself for a sea battle of epic proportions. Her knuckles went bone white where she gripped the wheel. She didn't move, didn't breathe until an answering shout rang out from the yacht.

"Ahoy, Lieutenant Escobar. Come aboard."

It took three fumbling tries, but she finally figured out how to cut the engine. Then there was nothing to do but hunker down, watch black-suited, heavily armed Navy SEALS scramble aboard the yacht and wait for rescue.

Not until Nina had clambered back aboard the yacht did she discover the reason Cordell and the Russians had given up without a battle.

"Has Cordell surrendered the disk?" she asked Wolf as he helped her from the bobbing launch.

"No." His jaw worked. "We seem to have a classic Mexican standoff."

"Huh?"

"You'll see."

He escorted her back to the main salon, where she found Cordell and a tall, wiry individual she guessed was Alekseev. They faced a black-suited and black-faced Mannie, a willowy blonde in a wet suit that fit her like a second skin, and an array of heavily armed Navy personnel. The tension was so heavy it almost hit Nina in the face, but—unbelievably!—Sebastian greeted her with a smile.

"Ah, there you are, my dear. I wondered where you'd hidden yourself." His smile grew somewhat strained. "I'm not surprised you were reluctant to face me after smashing my little nymph. How unfortunate that you injured one of my men in the process."

"*Most* unfortunate," she retorted. "I would have much preferred it had injured you."

"But why?" Sorrowfully, he shook his silver-maned head. "I offered you nothing but the hospitality of my home and my boat, which any number of witnesses will attest you accepted."

Incredulous, she gaped at him, at Wolf, at him again.

"You're kidding, right?"

"Not at all."

"This is the line you're taking?" She couldn't believe it! The man's gall was incredible. "You're suggesting we were *guests* aboard your little floating pleasure palace?"

"Not suggesting."

"You're crazy! You can't just shrug away the

bruise on Wolf's temple or the drug you pumped into me."

Sebastian shot his cuffs, looking coolly unperturbed. "Again, I can produce any number of witnesses who will confirm the man you introduced to me as your fiancé came aboard with that bruise. And if there are residual drugs in your system, I can only hope most sincerely that you kick whatever habit you've developed."

"Oh, for...!" Wolf slammed the handgun he'd taken from the downed henchman onto the bar counter. "Cut the crap, Cordell. You're not wiggling out of this one. You know damn well we've got the goods on you."

"Do you?" Calmly, he adjusted his cuff. "What goods, may I ask?"

"The encrypted disk you lifted from Senator DeWitt's office and sold to our friend here."

"Indeed? And where, precisely, is this disk?"

A muscle twitched in Wolf's jaw. Spotting it, Nina felt a sudden, hollow sensation in the pit of her stomach. He'd jumped back aboard the yacht, not just to cover her escape, she realized. He'd wanted—no, needed—to be in on the handover of the disk.

That, obviously, hadn't happened. And without the hard evidence linking Cordell to the stolen technology, the bastard might just wiggle off the hook after all.

"You're going to tell us where that disk is," Wolf warned, emanating promise and menace in equal measure.

"I can hardly tell you what I don't know."

The sheer arrogance of the man took Nina's breath away. Fist clenched, she stomped across the salon.

"Nina?"

Ignoring Wolf's questioning glance, she rounded the end of the bar.

"My dear!"

The wary note that leaped into Cordell's voice gave her a vicious satisfaction.

"What are you doing?"

"Treating myself to that drink you promised me. I think I've earned it, don't you?"

"Let me pour it for you."

Before he could take a step, she snatched the silver encrusted tequila bottle from its protective rack and whipped around.

"That's okay." She held the bottle up by its neck. "I'll pour my own."

Her eyes locked with Cordell's. She saw realization flare in his, felt triumph flood her own. Deliberately, Nina opened her fist.

"Ooops."

The two-thousand-dollar bottle shattered against the gleaming teak counter. Glass splintered and liquid spilled out, but the spiny silver plating held its shape. So did the medallion at its center. Which, Nina confirmed, with a blaze of satisfaction, was *not* made of bronze.

"Well, lookee here."

She poked carefully among the gooey shards and used a finger and thumbnail to lift the round, gray-colored object. Her glance swept the salon full of stunned personnel. She took almost as much pleasure from Alekseev's fierce scowl as from the red that now mottled Cordell's cheeks. The gleam of respect in the tall, slender blonde's eyes wasn't bad, either. But it was Wolf's crooked grin that put a silly smile on her face.

"I think this might be what you're looking for," she told him.

"I think it might."

Chapter 13

"I'm glad T.J. and I arrived in time to get in on the action," the long-legged blonde mused as she and Nina downed mugs of hot coffee and watched the sun come up from the forward deck of Cordell's yacht. "Been a while since we had this much fun."

The boat was on its way back to shore, minus its owner and about half the crew. They'd been hustled aboard the navy cutter that had come alongside several hours ago. Mannie had hauled Alekseev and his pals onto the cutter, too, citing violations to Mexico's gun laws and suspicious activity involving transfer of funds. A small contingent from Mexico's elite marine ops squad had remained aboard the yacht to bring it to safe anchorage at the police impound marina.

Wolf had gone with Mannie, along with a tall, well-muscled male in a black wetsuit. He'd turned out to be the husband of Nina's present companion, Jordan Colby, aka Diamond.

Diamond had traded her own wetsuit for a cool, cotton-weave robe appropriated from one of the yacht's well-supplied guest cabins. Beneath it she wore only the two-piece bathing suit she'd had on under the wetsuit. Nina had caught glimpses of the mile-long legs and slender body that had made the woman one of the highest-paid models in the world before she'd quit to begin designing her line of signature eyewear.

A pair of her sunglasses, with their distinctive butterfly logo, picked out in small diamonds in the corner of the left lens, rested on the bridge of her nose now. The sophisticated shades imbued Nina with intense envy and a firm resolve to order a pair as soon as she got home.

Home.

The very thought of it reverberated in her head. After last night, her condo nestled in the foothills of the Sandia Mountains beckoned like a shimmering oasis of peace and calm in an otherwise insane world. Sebastian Cordell and friends had maxed out Nina's newly awakened craving for excitement and danger. No way she could ever classify last night's terror "fun," the way Diamond just had.

"Tell me something." Cradling her coffee mug in both hands, she turned to the cool blonde. "You and T.J. work for the same agency that Wolf does. How often do you get tapped for assignments like this one?"

"It varies. Sometimes we go for months between ops. Other times, we might hop from one right into another."

"And you like living on the edge like that?"

"It certainly keeps life interesting." She slid her glasses down and tipped Nina a glance. "It's not for everyone, though."

"No kidding!"

Diamond hesitated, obviously choosing her words with care. "Look, it's obvious you and Wolf have something going on. If you're worried about getting in too deep, you might want to ask him how he came by his code name sometime."

"Thanks. I will."

Nina didn't tell her she was already in way over her head, but she couldn't help wondering what it would be like to live with a man who jumped into danger on a more or less regular basis. Could she lie awake night after night, wondering and worrying?

Not that Wolf asked her to do either. She was putting her own spin on his casual promise to come to Albuquerque when he'd wrapped things up down here.

Then again, Nina reminded herself, he'd made that promise while they still had some "unfinished business" from the beach to take care of. Maybe those two wild sessions at the Mayan Princess, before they'd left for the airport yesterday afternoon, had settled that score.

She didn't *think* so, but the uncertainty gnawed at her so much that she was only marginally grateful, once back on dry land, to find that Mannie's people had recovered her luggage from the hijacked rental car. They had no idea what had happened to her straw tote, however. So her first act was to borrow Diamond's cell phone to cancel her credit cards and notify the on-call duty officer at the U.S. Consulate in Cabo San Lucas that she'd lost her passport.

"They want me to come by and fill out an application for a replacement passport."

"Not a problem," Diamond assured her. "Let's get changed. We can swing by the consulate on our way to rendezvous with the guys."

Diamond and her husband had left their gear

at Wolf's hotel. They'd checked his room after verifying that he and Nina had departed the Mayan, then failed to show at the airport. At that point, she and T.J. had contacted Mannie Diaz and joined the naval assault team.

"How did you get in?" Nina wanted to know as she and Diamond swept past the front desk of the hotel overlooking the sea. The Pacifica was several steps down from the ultra-fashionable Mayan Princess, but bursting with color and fragrant with the scent of bougainvillea.

"OMEGA operatives have their ways of accessing hotel rooms," Diamond said with a smile as she zapped the key code on the door to Wolf's.

Once inside the functional one-bedroom minisuite, Nina looked around with interest. Rafe Blackstone certainly wasn't the neatest person in the world. The desk chair sported the wrinkled and very gaudy tropical shirt he'd had on the night they'd met at the marina. The knit polo he'd worn to lunch with Cordell lay crumpled at the foot of the bed. A beat-up leather carryall spilling a variety of electronic implements sat atop a dresser.

Diamond set her small overnighter on the desk. "You want first dibs on the shower?"

Nina wanted out of her wrinkled linen slacks and red tank in the worst way, but another urgent priority had surfaced. She tried to remember when she'd last eaten and came up blank.

"You go ahead. I'm famished. While you do your thing, I'll hit the café and order two breakfasts to go."

"Sounds good." Diamond fished a wad of pesos out of her sleek designer handbag. "Better take these, since you're cash- and credit-cardless."

Nina felt a little weird as she strolled the palm-shaded walk that wound between the detached units. After days of looking over her shoulder and playing to a listening device and getting kidnapped not once, but twice, she experienced a relieved, if slightly nervous, sense of freedom. Her stomach provided a distraction as she approached the crowded café and caught her first whiff of sizzling sausage and spicy huevos rancheros. Unfortunately, she'd timed her expedition at the height of the breakfast hour. It took almost a half hour to get a carry-out order.

Balancing a heavy sack and two tall cups of coffee, she made her way back along the palm-shaded walk. With both hands full, she had to kick the door panel to get Diamond's attention. But when the door swung open a few seconds later, the individual on the other side was neither blonde nor freshly showered.

"Wolf!"

He looked rumpled and red-eyed from lack of sleep, with dark bristles shading his cheeks and chin. The bruise on his temple had turned an ugly purplish green. Yet the grin he gave her was all male, and so potent that Nina's heart skipped several beats.

"Diamond indicated we would rendezvous with you and her husband downtown," she said a little breathlessly.

"That was the plan." He relieved her of the precariously balanced coffees. "But it looks like the wrap-up will take longer than expected. So we decided to take a break, clean up, and start fresh later this afternoon."

She trailed him into the minisuite and looked around. "Where are your friends?"

"They went to the front desk to get their own room." He set the cups on the desk and reached for the paper sack. His blue eyes held hers. "They have to stay for wrap-up, but they plan to fly back tonight, if possible. Diamond offered to take you to the consulate to get a replacement passport so you could leave with them. I told them I'd take care of all that. Later."

Oooh-kay.

"If that's all right by you," he added with a

totally unconvincing show of willingness to defer to her wishes in the matter.

"Well..."

"Good. That's settled. Let's eat. I'm starving."

They took their breakfast to the suite's small balcony and ate from the cartons. The double order of beans and huevos rancheros disappeared in quick, hungry forkfuls. So did the warm, sugar-dusted *sopapillas* slathered with butter and honey. Washed down by gulps of coffee, it was hands-down the best meal Nina had ever consumed.

The absence of nerve-crawling tension added to her enjoyment, of course. Then there was the company. He sat across from her, still rumpled and red-eyed and unshaven, but looking totally relaxed...until he caught her gaze.

Eyes narrowed, he searched her face. "You sure you're all right? No lingering aftereffects from the stuff Cordell's goons pumped into you?"

"Not that I can tell."

"I was ready to kill him when I came to. I came close, very close, just before you showed up in the salon."

A shudder rippled down Nina's spine. Sitting here in the bright sunlight made the terror of the night before seem even darker and more desperate.

"The worst of it is that I didn't tell you..."

Scowling, Wolf scraped a palm across his chin. "That is, I didn't let you know…"

"What?"

His frown deepened. "Do you remember me telling you how I felt when I saw you charging down the alleyway?"

Like she could forget it? "As if the ground had dropped out from under you."

"Right. Well, take that feeling and multiply it by a thousand," he said with grim emphasis, "and you might come close to how I felt last night."

She caught her breath. Was he trying to say what she thought he was?

"I'm sorry I dragged you into this mess, Nina."

The air left her lungs with a whoosh. "That's what you've been leading up to? An apology?"

Shoving back his chair, he took her hand and tugged her up to stand beside him on the narrow balcony.

"I'm *trying* to say I love you."

Well! That was better.

"I know it's too soon," he said gruffly, sliding his arms around her waist. "We haven't really had time to get to know each other and you're still getting over the hurt from your jerk of a fiancé."

"What fiancé?"

A sense of absolute rightness filled her heart as she framed his bristly cheeks with both hands.

"I dated Kevin for almost a year before we got engaged, and look what a disaster that turned out to be. I've known you for, what? Five days? Yet I know all I need to about you. No, wait! There is one thing."

"What's that?"

"Diamond told me to ask you how you came by your code name."

A rueful smile tipped his lips. "She did, huh?"

"She did. What's that all about?"

"Most wolves run in packs, but I've always preferred to operate independently. No ties, no entanglements."

"I assume that includes women."

"It did." His arms tightened, pulling her closer. "Until now."

She could feel him hardening against her belly. Her pulse leaped in response, but the doubts that had pinged her earlier came creeping back.

"We need to talk about those ties, Wolf. I'm not sure how well I would do, sitting home and chewing on my fingernails while you go off to battle the Cordells and Alekseevs of the world."

He brushed back a strand of tangled hair. "Someone has to do it."

"True."

"But I've been thinking about that, too. Even lone wolves need to come in from the cold eventually. I've been with OMEGA ten years now. It may be time to take a break, work on other interests. See what new directions life takes."

"That," she breathed, sliding her arms around his neck, "sounds like an excellent idea."

"And in the meantime..." He dropped a fierce kiss on her mouth. "A quick shower and a good three or four hours of sack time might be in order."

"Might, hell!"

Their shower turned out to be anything but quick. Wolf soaped her down, up, and down again. Nina returned the favor, deriving intensely erotic pleasure from the glide of her hand over his taut muscles and slick skin.

And when he lifted her, hooked her legs around his waist, and thrust into her, she knew most definitely her wolf had come in from the cold.

* * * * *

COMING NEXT MONTH

Available June 29, 2010

ROMANTIC SUSPENSE

SRCCNM0610

REQUEST YOUR FREE BOOKS!

2 FREE NOVELS PLUS 2 FREE GIFTS!

ROMANTIC SUSPENSE

Sparked by Danger, Fueled by Passion.

YES! Please send me 2 FREE Silhouette® Romantic Suspense novels and my 2 FREE gifts (gifts are worth about $10). After receiving them, if I don't wish to receive any more books, I can return the shipping statement marked "cancel." If I don't cancel, I will receive 4 brand-new novels every month and be billed just $4.24 per book in the U.S. or $4.99 per book in Canada. That's a saving of 15% off the cover price! It's quite a bargain! Shipping and handling is just 50¢ per book.* I understand that accepting the 2 free books and gifts places me under no obligation to buy anything. I can always return a shipment and cancel at any time. Even if I never buy another book from Silhouette, the two free books and gifts are mine to keep forever.

240/340 SDN E5Q4

Name	(PLEASE PRINT)	
Address		Apt. #
City	State/Prov.	Zip/Postal Code

Signature (if under 18, a parent or guardian must sign)

Mail to the Silhouette Reader Service:
IN U.S.A.: P.O. Box 1867, Buffalo, NY 14240-1867
IN CANADA: P.O. Box 609, Fort Erie, Ontario L2A 5X3

Not valid for current subscribers to Silhouette Romantic Suspense books.

**Want to try two free books from another line?
Call 1-800-873-8635 or visit www.morefreebooks.com.**

* Terms and prices subject to change without notice. Prices do not include applicable taxes. N.Y. residents add applicable sales tax. Canadian residents will be charged applicable provincial taxes and GST. Offer not valid in Quebec. This offer is limited to one order per household. All orders subject to approval. Credit or debit balances in a customer's account(s) may be offset by any other outstanding balance owed by or to the customer. Please allow 4 to 6 weeks for delivery. Offer available while quantities last.

Your Privacy: Silhouette is committed to protecting your privacy. Our Privacy Policy is available online at www.eHarlequin.com or upon request from the Reader Service. From time to time we make our lists of customers available to reputable third parties who may have a product or service of interest to you. If you would prefer we not share your name and address, please check here. ☐

Help us get it right—We strive for accurate, respectful and relevant communications. To clarify or modify your communication preferences, visit us at www.ReaderService.com/consumerchoice.

SRS10R

HARLEQUIN®

A Romance

FOR EVERY MOOD™

Spotlight on

Heart & Home

Heartwarming romances
where love can happen
right when you least expect it.

See the next page to enjoy a sneak peek
from Silhouette Special Edition®,
a Heart and Home series.

*Introducing MCFARLANE'S PERFECT BRIDE
by USA TODAY bestselling author Christine Rimmer,
from Silhouette Special Edition®.*

Entranced. Captivated. Enchanted.

Connor sat across the table from Tori Jones and couldn't help thinking that those words exactly described what effect the small-town schoolteacher had on him. He might as well stop trying to tell himself he wasn't interested. He was powerfully drawn to her.

Clearly, he should have dated more when he was younger.

There had been a couple of other women since Jennifer had walked out on him. But he had never been entranced. Or captivated. Or enchanted.

Until now.

He wanted her—*her,* Tori Jones, in particular. Not just someone suitably attractive and well-bred, as Jennifer had been. Not just someone sophisticated, sexually exciting and discreet, which pretty much described the two women he'd dated after his marriage crashed and burned.

It came to him that he...he *liked* this woman. And that was new to him. He liked her quick wit, her wisdom and her big heart. He liked the passion in her voice when she talked about things she believed in.

He liked *her.* And suddenly it mattered all out of proportion that she might like him, too.

Was he losing it? He couldn't help but wonder. Was he cracking under the strain—of the soured economy, the McFarlane House setbacks, his divorce, the scary changes in his son? Of the changes he'd decided he needed to make in his life and himself?

Strangely, right then, on his first date with Tori Jones, he didn't care if he just might be going over the edge. He was having a great time—having *fun*, of all things—and he didn't want it to end.

Is Connor finally able to admit his feelings to Tori, and are they reciprocated?
Find out in MCFARLANE'S PERFECT BRIDE by USA TODAY bestselling author Christine Rimmer. Available July 2010, only from Silhouette Special Edition®.

Bestselling Harlequin Presents® author
Penny Jordan
brings you an exciting new trilogy...

Needed:
THE WORLD'S MOST
ELIGIBLE
BILLIONAIRES

Three penniless sisters:
how far will they go to save the ones they love?

Lizzie, Charley and Ruby refuse to drown in their debts.
And three of the richest, most ruthless men in the world
are about to enter their lives. Pure, proud but penniless,
how far will these sisters go to save the ones they love?

Look out for

Lizzie's story—**THE WEALTHY GREEK'S
CONTRACT WIFE,** July

Charley's story—**THE ITALIAN DUKE'S
VIRGIN MISTRESS,** August

Ruby's story—**MARRIAGE: TO CLAIM HIS TWINS,**
September

www.eHarlequin.com

HP12927

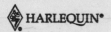